# SIGN ON FOR TOKYO

# SIGN ON
# FOR TOKYO

## Alec Haig

DODD, MEAD & COMPANY
New York

This book is dedicated to Jane Eustace; to Arai-san, Katsuhiro Kurata, and Nakai-san, who will never forgive the liberties I take with their wonderful country; and to a man called Gerry, who handed me my first piece of blue glass and told me to look into the heart of a Bessemer. That is fact – the rest, I hope, fiction.

# SIGN ON FOR TOKYO

# UNFINISHED BUSINESS

... Alec Haig's New York address was on West Eleventh Street, near enough the village to be inconspicuously bohemian, far enough from the beatniks of Washington Square to be respectable. The apartment was what the realtors call a two-and-a-half roomer, though Alec had never known whether the half was the bathroom, too small even to hold a bath, or the bedroom, too voluptuously decorated to hold anything but a six-feet-square bed and a bedside table the size and height for a brandy bottle and a glass, a pack of cigarettes and an ash-tray. The Instecon company apartment, to which Alec was entitled, was on Sutton Place South with a view of the East River, three guest bedrooms, a sitting-room large enough for a Lions Convention, décor by Heimbrecker of Park Avenue, and a Puerto Rican maid willing to oblige any member of the company management who asked her. Alec Haig preferred his West Eleventh Street pad. He had arrived from Kennedy Airport less than a half-hour ago, on the flight from Los Angeles. Among its other American subsidiaries, Instecon had an aircraft company tucked behind the Topanga Canyon making wingless aircraft no one outside Instecon was supposed to know anything about. The previous week, Alec had been shown a drawing of one of these aircraft in the apartment of a young girl in Amsterdam. His telephone bell rang with the call to the head office in Zürich. He had a harmless-sounding conversation with Françoise, the words

1

endearing as Françoise told him, several times, how much she missed him. While they were talking, Alec played the tape with the real message on it, over the same telephone through a mixing and coding amplifier. The telephone call ended, he took a shower, and dressed in a black mohair suit, a white button-down collar, and a dark crimson shot-silk tie. He grimaced as he caught sight of the tie in the mirror. 'When in Rome . . .' he said. He slipped into his pocket a silver cigarette-case and lighter, a lawn handkerchief, a bill-fold containing a thousand dollars, and a Universal credit card in the name of Alec Haig, with no company countersignature, known to be available to private citizens only on evidence of a substantial cash balance in the bank. It was recognized everywhere as proof of financial respectability. He left the apartment, and walked along West Eleventh Street east to Fifth Avenue. There he signalled the first cab that came along. The cab took him north up Fifth, then ran down Forty-Eighth Street to a small French restaurant, Le Chat Méchant. He ordered a meal of *pâté maison*, *le coq au vin*, and a lemon ice, with a half bottle of Grands Echézeaux, 1957. He was drinking a brandy when Gene McGurney slipped into the seat beside him. Gene, all of two hundred and fifty pounds, was sweating profusely.

'Couldn't find a lousy cab!' he said.

'Think nothing of it, my dear chap,' Alec said.

'It was a tough assignment,' Gene said – then 'Gimme a bourbon on the rocks,' he said to the passing waitress – 'and I'm up to my neck in it, so don't make waves! The guy you want is Lou Bradley. He used to work for NBS-TV, but they found him with his hand up the wrong broad's skirts! She was getting laid by someone from the top of the tower!'

'You put it so delicately, Gene,' Alec said.

'Aw, hell, it was no secret!'

2

Gene was top electronics man for the Consolidated Broad-casting Network, with affiliated stations throughout America. In his spare time a radio amateur passionately interested in electronics and communication, he had designed a network of communications satellites to work in conjunction with the Early Bird system. He would have been in Washington had he not once told a visiting President to stop talking such crap!

The waitress brought his bourbon on the rocks, and Gene downed it in one gulp. 'That sure hits the spot!' he said. 'Now bring me another, just like it, and we'll do a little social drinking!'

'You said it was a difficult assignment, if I remember correctly, and told me not to make waves, which I believe means don't stir up any trouble for you.'

'That's right. Lou Bradley. He's mean. He went sour after the networks closed up on him. Word around is that he's turned bad, very bad!'

'How bad?'

Gene looked apprehensively around the restaurant, then lowered his voice. 'They say he's operating the Network spread all over America! But they can never nail him with anything subversive.'

Alec hid his quickening interest. 'Where will I find Lou Bradley?' he asked.

'El Morocco, The Forum, right across the road, the Copa, Basin Street East – you name it, that's where you'll find him – but I warn you, he's a bad one.'

'How bad?' Alec's voice became crisp. 'This word bad you keep using, it tells me nothing.'

'Does this tell you anything – they say a couple of guys wound up in the river – so, like I say, don't make waves.'

Alec made two telephone calls when Gene left.

3

As Alec went into the glittering Acapulco Room he held out his hand to the *maître d'hôtel*. In it was a twenty-dollar bill. Without even glancing down, he started to show Alec through the crowds to the centre of the bandstand, clicking his fingers to a waiter who grasped a spare table and started to carry it over the heads of the diners already packed like sardines. Alec took the *maître d*'s arm and beckoned to a seat just below the bar from which he could see all the room, but no one standing at the bar could look down on him.

Frances Faye was performing in the cabaret, making her usual suggestive insults to her superb bass-player. 'Once you've had me, you'll never want another,' she said, between songs. It drew its usual laugh from the cocktail-happy matrons sitting with plastic smiles and genuine diamonds below her. 'Lou Bradley,' Alec said to the *maître d'hôtel*.

'He might be in later, there's one of his men in the bar. Would you like to speak to him?'

Alec nodded and the *maître d'* went quickly up the short flight of stairs to the bar. When the man came down Alec stood up and invited him to sit.

'My name is Alec Haig,' he said, 'and I'm particularly anxious to see Lou Bradley tonight.'

'He's not here,' the man said.

'I know he's not here, but I wondered if you know where I can find him.'

'Are you the law?' the man said.

Alec shook his head.

'Give me a card or something!' the man said.

Alec took out his Universal credit card. The man whistled when he saw it. 'He's at the Cowboy Room. Third Avenue. Just north of United Nations building.'

The Cowboy Room had been designed for advertising

agents seeking an instant reputation for manliness. The door-keeper's ride 'em cowboy's outfit had seen every circus and film set on the east coast. Lou Bradley had a table all to himself – except for four girls of different coloured hair but equal ambitions. When Alec sat down, Lou quietly told them to powder their noses. Alec refused a drink. 'Shan't be staying long, old man,' he said, his voice a deliberate English drawl. 'They tell me you've been a naughty boy!'

Lou looked, as well he might do, perplexed. No one talked to Lou like that any more. 'Come to the point, Fauntleroy!' he said.

'You've been operating a network,' Alec said; 'stealing information that doesn't belong to you, and transmitting it round the world. Now, I don't care about other people's information, but when you start your nasty little game with information belonging to my company, that annoys me.'

Now Lou had him placed. He looked across at the bar and winked at a man standing with two other men there. If Alec noticed, he gave no sign, but carried on talking, unperturbed. 'The information you've been passing round the world is strictly business information and to keep the authorities off your track you've avoided government secrets like the plague.'

'That's right,' Lou said '– so there's not a thing you or anyone else can do about it!'

'On the contrary,' Alec said. He looked at his watch. 'Your network has just finished transmitting from Los Angeles the secret process for manufacturing the additives to the oxygen system of the Delta V anti-missile missile, and that particular transmission has been monitored by the FBI in every office in this country. It was an all-stations message, so all your contacts have run it, including the Russian and the Chinese – against, I might add, Federal Regulations. Of course, the information was coded to read like business information on the manufacture of carbon dioxide for a soft drinks plant.'

Lou laughed. 'What an imagination,' he said, 'what an imagination! My network has no man operating in any government plant in Los Alamos.'

Alec Haig took his cigarette case from his inside pocket, and speaking directly into it he said, 'It's all right. I've had my five minutes. Three at the bar you might look at.' He pressed down the catch on the side of the cigarette case. 'Useful little gadgets,' he said. 'They transmit for half a mile.' Lou started to rise in his chair, but at that moment the door opened and six men came in. They had the close-cropped look of football forwards, Yale graduates, FBI men.

'Before they get here,' Alec said, 'I'd like you to know we fed your man that information, and he fell for it, but you'll never be able to prove it. The FBI will smash your entire organization, destroy you all like so many rodents.'

Lou reached inside his jacket, but before he could draw the gun Alec reached out and grasped his arm, above the bones of his wrist. He tightened the pincer-like grip and pulled Lou's hand down, away from the shoulder holster. Lou was powerless to move. The sweat stood out on his forehead as he tried to lift his arm. No one at any of the adjacent tables had any idea of the struggle taking place. Slowly Alec pushed downwards until Lou was compelled to sit back in his seat, his numbed hand useless on the table before him. 'I hate violence,' Alec said.

The FBI men had spread out along the bar. Two of them detached themselves from the group and came across to the

6

table. 'All the stations ran it,' the first FBI man said. 'Now we have a case against the entire network!'

'Good,' Alec said. 'We were going to change that oxygen system tomorrow morning.'

INSTECON

INTERNAL MEMORANDUM DISTRIBUTION A. ONLY

From: Head of Accounts
To:   Head of Tech. Sales (Misc.)

We refer to your last expenses voucher and
item seventeen on page two (fee to T. C.
Pappayannikas for manufacture of one gun).
Since it was expressly agreed that funds
would not be forthcoming for the purchase or
manufacture of aggressive weapons, the
function of Tech. Sales (Misc.) being purely
defensive, we would be grateful if you
would explain this item. We are, meanwhile,
disallowing the sum of seventeen pounds ten
shillings (sterling equivalent) from the
total.

J. C. Crump. Head of
Accounts

INSTECON

INTERNAL MEMORANDUM DISTRIBUTION A. ONLY

From: Head of Tech. Sales (Misc.)
To:   Head of Accounts.

My dear Crump,
If only you'd read the report, you'd see why
this special gun was needed. If you don't
intend to read the reports, don't ask for a
carbon copy!

Alec Haig
Head of Tech. Sales (Misc.)

An industrial espionage agent who
tries to expose a network transmitting
secret steel processes comes face to
face with murder.

# PHASE I

It was dark in the valley, a darkness made more intense by sporadic illumination from the eye-blasting roaring tongue of flame as the Bessemer Converters were blown, the coke oven tapped, and quenched. These infrequent but regular gouts of heat and light singed the eyes, and blackened the darkness that followed. Men set their watches by it, with an intimate knowledge of the steel-making processes – 'Blowing Number Two extra tonight, must be a lot of sulphur – Number Three's a bit blue in the flame, must be that Swedish ore.' And then the light would go out and the heat melt away, and the valley be left again to darkness and repose.

A man crossed the open ground between the railway line and the back wall of the steel-making plant, by the Bessemers. He was a small man, but broad, wearing a black track suit, and rope-soled shoes. In his hands he carried what appeared to be a flat square box, the metal painted black. His eyes glittered through a Balaclava hood. The hood too was black. His soft leather gloves were black. He crossed the open ground quickly, confidently, and reached the corrugated iron wall of the Bessemer plant. When he got there he pressed himself against the wall, beside a steel girder that rose sheer into the air. He opened the box he carried. Inside was a network of steel tubing. He unfolded four spikes set into the lid, to project under the box. He put the box on the ground, stood on the lid to drive in the four spikes. He grasped the knob on the side of the box and turned it. There was an almost inaudible sound of air and the steel tubes started to rise from the box, up the side of the building, taking a tubing crosspiece with them every twelve inches. Within a minute he had erected a ladder of steel tubes silently against the corrugated iron. The ladder was black. Quickly he mounted it, carrying with him a thin wire. At the top of the building he squatted on the roof and pressed a switch on the thin wire. The ladder quickly descended under the release of the compressed air until it was back in the black box, almost invisible. The man crossed the roof on his knees, moving quickly as a cat and as gracefully. When he got to the far side of the roof, where it joined the gantry, he slid himself around the scaffolding supporting the corrugated iron and began a slow descent down the inner face of the wall. The scaffolding was strengthened by cross-bracing pieces of tubing. He slid carefully down each piece until he reached the floor below. He crossed the Bessemer platform to where a small door was set in an inner wall, stood in the entrance, and then he waited. This is the moment, he thought. This is the point to which all your efforts, all your skill, all your loyalties, bring you. The physical effort of getting there was never much of a trial – he could scale a wall as easily as the average man could climb a staircase. He could hang by his arms and traverse a wire, if the wire were strong enough to hold him. But there always came a time when the physical part was half over, when you were in. Then you had to do what you came for, and you had to do it correctly and swiftly. But however much you may plan every move you made, there was never a time when all the danger could be planned out of whatever you were doing. There never was a clean job. Take this job. Get inside, do what you had to do, and get out again. He had planned how to get inside, and by planning had removed all the problems.

He had planned how to get out again, and there were no problems there. But the bit in the middle, that was the bit he'd had to leave to chance. As long as the men were blowing steel there was a chance someone would come into that office. Once the steel was blown the men would go down the iron stairs at the other end of the platform to snatch a quick cup of tea. Thank God for compulsive tea drinkers. So, he dare not go into the office while they were on the platform blowing. But he couldn't delay his climb. If he were not on the platform by the time they started a blow, there was a chance one of them would come out at the back and see him scaling the wall. Too much tea again, and the men's toilet a couple of hundred yards away. And so, he had to leave the centre bit, the bit between coming and going, to chance. And that he didn't like. It wasn't clean. No professional would like it.

On the other side of the platform, about twenty feet distant, but around a corner from him, the crew were preparing a Bessemer for blowing. The vast cup, twenty or more feet high, was swung into the vertical position, containing its iron from the re-heating furnace. Then the steel maker opened the blowing valve. There was a sudden roaring within the huge cup, and a jet of flame, eight or nine feet long, intense in heat and light. The roaring lasted only a couple of minutes. Each of the five men on the steel maker's platform looked at the flame through blue glass held in three-inch by four-inch wooden frames they held before their faces like masks. The chief steel maker raised his arm. His first assistant kept his hands on the wheel controlling the blower. Another assistant stood at the electric panel which activated the tipping mechanism. When the steel maker was satisfied with the colour of the flame, when his lifetime of experience, his sensing, could know that the steel was 'right' he brought down his arm rapidly. The first assistant cut the air blower, the second assistant pressed the tilt button, and quickly the whole of the counterbalanced Bessemer cup tilted forward until the steel master could look down inside it. He took his blue glass again before his face and looked intently at the bubbling surface of the slag on the top of the molten metal within the cup. Another assistant came forward with a long pole with a ladle on its end. He dipped this long spoon into the Bessemer and drew out a spoonful of the molten metal. He tipped the spoon on the Bessemer platform. The metal ran out into a box. The steel master peered at it again through his blue glass. It cooled rapidly. He tipped over the box and the metal, already solid on its outside, fell out as a cake. He hit the cake with a hammer. Bits of the slag broke from it. Everyone was tense, awaiting his decision. Then he gave a thumbs-up sign, the second assistant touched a button and the Bessemer continued its downwards tilt. The molten slag poured off the top of the metal first into a truck waiting below. The truck was moved out of position, another came along the rails to take its place and the whole contents of the Bessemer were allowed to run out into the truck. As they ran out a workman ran forward and sprinkled a powder on to the surface. Sparks jumped from the truck as he sprinkled. A man standing at the side of the Bessemer platform had a sheaf of papers on a clipboard before him. On a control panel on the wall the needles of pyrometers and recording instruments had flickered as the steel had been blown. From time to time he had jotted down figures on his pad. A clock ticked away on the top of the panel, a clock with a large seconds sweep hand. The man looked at his instruments, satisfied with the priceless secrets they yielded to him. But in his satisfaction was more than just pleasure at a scientific result. There was also an atmosphere of triumph, a secret ring of triumph about him, that most revealed itself when, without

14

knowing, the steel master had called the 'blow' order exactly at the moment the clock on the panel of instruments registered zero.

The man in the doorway, wearing black, waited until the light had completely died away, until the platform was illuminated only by the working lights and the bright red glow of the metal in the tub below and then he opened the door behind him and went inside the office.

From an inside pocket of his track suit he produced a small camera, no bigger than a matchbox. The light in the office was sufficient for highly sensitive film. He opened the file which lay on the table. On the top of the first page was written, in a bold hand, 'Notes on P-less Steel', below it the crossbow insignia of the International Steel Consortium. He took off his Balaclava helmet and held the camera to his eye, photographing the title page first. He turned the pages over rapidly, pausing only to take a quickly shot of each posed. He had just finished the last shot when the door opened. A workman from the Bessemer platform was standing in the doorway. In his hand he carried on a clipboard the carbon copies of the documents being photographed.

'What are *you* doing in here?' he asked, surprised identification showing on his face.

The man put down his camera and walked slowly forward. The workman came into the room. When he was clear of the doorway the man leaped. He turned the flattened palm of his hand upwards and when exactly within reach, he shot his hand and arm sideways. The blow took the workman by surprise in the space at the bottom of his throat immediately below his Adam's apple. He tried to speak but couldn't. Then he started to fall. The intruder leaped silently to the side of him and with one movement caught him as he was falling and shut the door. The workman lay on the floor. The man lifted one eyelid, satisfied that the workman was dead. No one could survive a blow such as that one. He went back to the folder on the table and rearranged it as it had formerly been. He picked up his camera, wound the film onward, opened the back and extracted the tiny capsule of exposed film. He put the film in one pocket, the camera in the other. He crossed to the door, turned, and with a professional's eye verified he had left no trace of his presence, other than the dead body at his feet. He opened the door. No one was outside. He bent down and with surprising strength picked up the workman and carried him out of the office. He paused, his eyes accustoming themselves to the comparative gloom of the platform. Then he grasped the dead man in both hands, one on the leg and one on the shoulder and in a lithe semi-run he loped to the edge of the platform and threw the dead man with all his strength. The dead man went over the rail at the edge of the platform and through the air into the vat of molten steel. There was a cloud of steam, smoke, and the surface of the steel was covered in flames. By this time the intruder had scaled the inside of the corrugated iron-clad scaffolding and was crouched on the roof. There was no disturbance below. He crossed the roof, found the end of the wire where he had hung it, and pressed the switch. The steel ladder came twisting up the wall under the pressure of compressed air. Without even testing it, for he knew its strength, he climbed over the edge of the roof and slid down the ladder without bothering to put his feet on to each rung. Once down he opened the release mechanism, the ladder descended and he packed it away into his box and vanished into the darkness. Ten minutes later, he walked into the steel works through the front gate.

'Good night, sir,' the gate-man said.

Outside the canteen, Joe Michaels from the steel sheet

plant was returning to his shift. As he passed the canteen window his fingers idly slid along the under side of the frame. When he placed his hand in his pocket, the capsule of film was in it. Inside the steel sheet dispatch department he went across to the strapping machine which already contained a consignment of steel sheets, labelled and ready to go when strapped. It was the last job he had done before going for supper. He slid the film capsule into the feed end of the strapping machine, beneath the steel tape. He then pulled the ratchet handle until the steel straps were taut on the sheet. He locked the clipping arm into position and pulled the clipping lever. A copper clip was formed around the steel straps and tensed into position. The steel strap was severed just after the fastening. He pulled the bale of sheets out of the strapping machine, and examined the copper fastenings. No one could have known that the one nearest to him contained a tube of micro-film. Joe Michaels signalled for the fork-lift truck driver, who lifted the bale of steel sheets with his fork-lift truck and ran them to the door of the packing department. A lorry was parked there. He hoisted the package high, and dropped it on the floor of the truck, behind the rest of the load.

'That's your lot then,' he said to the driver.

The driver ticked the last entry on his load sheet, got into the cabin, and started the lorry. At the main gate the checker came out. 'When was you last searched?' the checker asked.

'Last night.'

'Are you sure? I can check it!'

'I know you can check it!'

'Right – you can get on your way.'

The driver gave a sigh of relief as he engaged the gear and drove through the gates. Checks were severe at International

Steel Consortium. Not the routine matter they had been in the past, when the gate police were looking for anything you'd knocked off to help build your chicken run. Now you could neither get in nor out of Instecon without running the risk of being stripped to the skin and examined under infra-red, ultra-violet, and X-ray eyes. And the damn searches could delay a man something cruel. He had to be up in Prestwick for that first delivery early in the morning, and then he had to drop off near Glasgow after that. He drove the lorry north for the Heads of the Valley road. Thank God for the motorways, he thought, as he drove into the black black night.

Steel Fabricators Limited of Prestwick was housed in a small building near the perimeter of the airport, an unprepossessing one-storey construction – not that that bothered the driver. You took your invoices and your load, and you delivered wherever it said on the invoice. You made certain of getting a signature on the copy invoice, and then as fast as possible you were on your way again, and that's all there was to it.

As the lorry drove out of the gate eyes watched from behind the office window. A telephone call was made, to an innocent-looking office over the street carrying no name. The band around the steel sheets was cut. The copper fastening, carefully prised open, revealed the capsule of micro-film, un-damaged. The micro-film capsule was taken, tightly held in the hand of the man who signed the invoice. Before crossing the road he looked carefully up and down. There appeared no unusual activity. Other eyes were watching from the second storey of the office building, eyes that had been watching long before the lorry arrived. The light in that room was switched on momentarily, then switched off again. The man crossed the road and sauntered into the office building.

Once inside, he handed the capsule over to another man who took it up the stairs. In the small back room was a photographic laboratory and equipment. Within twenty minutes the film had been processed. The first frame was loaded into a projector, and the image cast on to a white screen. It was a perfect representation of the front page of 'Notes on P-less Steel'. The Crossbow of International Steel Consortium showed particularly crisply. The man who had processed the film picked up the telephone in the projection room.

'Ready,' he said.

The telephone call to Basle was established almost as quickly as a dialled call to the same town. When the call came, the line was crisp and clear. The industrial camera in Prestwick was switched on. The reproduction of the front page of the Notes came up sharply on the television monitor. The electrical signal from the camera was fed into a special amplifier, and a switch was pressed connecting that amplifier's output with the telephone. In Basle, the Swiss operator started his tape recorder. The signal came in from England, like the tuneless moaning sound of a musical saw. The same sequence of sound was repeated over and over again. When the operator had recorded it a number of times he stopped the tape recorder. He glanced at his watch. Five seconds to go. Meanwhile in Prestwick the picture before the television camera had been changed. The switch connecting the amplifier to the telephone was pressed exactly on the five seconds mark, and the musical saw sound began again. Page by page the Notes on P-less Steel were transmitted down the telephone wire each five seconds turning the pages as easily as one would turn the pages of a book. Anyone accidentally listening to that telephone call would have thought the sound an atmospheric, that the two communicants had not yet come on the line. Within forty-five seconds the whole of the contents of the micro-film had been transmitted and the micro-film itself destroyed.

'If we put an automatic changer on the film frames we could change those pictures every two seconds,' the Scottish operator said. 'That way we'd get the entire call over in fifteen seconds. It'd be a lot safer, and we'd save money, too!'

In Basle, Hans Grotau was on the telephone to Seattle, Washington, in the United States of America. Oddly enough, when the telephone call came through, he didn't say a word. There were twenty seconds of the musical-saw sound and then silence. In Seattle, Lew Allen had placed a telephone call to Tokyo, Japan. And he didn't talk, either.

In the Mitziguchi Steel Works just outside Tokyo, was a small room, the existence of which was known only to a few of the chief executives. On the door were the Japanese symbols which meant, 'Do Not Disturb'. Below that the sign for 'Entry Forbidden'. Inside the small room was a complex of radio and television facilities. From that small room it was possible for Kotaro Hitohori to speak, should he be so rash, to the entire world. Certainly, in that small room it was possible for him to listen to the entire world. On the shelf behind his desk were the volumes of all the known business codes used in sending industrial information in secret throughout the world. A row of operatives on the far wall, each wearing headphones, tuned in to telex systems operating through the entire world, listening, noting, frequently tape recording. The quick fingers sped along knobs, tuning here, trimming there, searching, constantly searching the radio ether for an elusive sound, the tip tap of a morse code transmitter. From frequent listening, the operators had familiarized themselves with the exact note of every transmitter in which they had a special interest. Their main targets were the telex

20

transmitting stations, that send information of all kinds from country to country. And their main interest was company information, commercial indiscretions which could yield as much information as a look inside the locked drawers of the desk of the Managing Director. Every signal that came into this pulsing listening station, this open ear, was recorded on tape. Important messages were copied off the tape, and transcribed for de-coding.

The Brazil office of Fabricantos Sintéticos S.A. of Barcelona is asking how much to quote for 2,000 tons of steel to be used for building a bridge over the Guadalcante. Another operator monitored the reply from Barcelona. Offer at 1,549 pesetas, plus 5 per cent plus 5 per cent. Señor Don Garcia Gomez, the purchasing agent, wants two weeks in Miami, Florida, and a Cadillac motor car for his mother for the pleasure of viewing our quotation. Granted, came back from Barcelona. These facts and figures were quickly typed in the form of a digest and handed to Kotaro Hitohori. With an authority second only to the Managing Director, Kotaro Hitohori punched a card and slipped it into a small computer whose mechanism was built into the walls of his office. He handed the resulting paper to the South American operator, who encoded it and put it out on the teleprinter to the Brazil office. Offer at 1,535 pesetas equivalent, contact a Señor Don Garcia Gomez and offer him two weeks in Miami, a Rolls-Royce for his mother and an E-type Jaguar for himself. And find out whom he knows in Miami, just in case he gets lonely at night.

Kotaro Hitohori was well trained for this work. A steel man by training, the start of the last war had found him in the Ruhr, studying, and sending back to Tokyo for copying, the latest steel-making techniques. When the war came, uncertain of the position that Japan would take, he fled to

England where he continued his steel studies. The opportunities for transmitting information back to Japan, however, were limited. When it became apparent that anyone of Japanese nationality would not be welcome in England, he travelled first to Switzerland and then to Sweden. Sweden was the centre of the pro-Axis information net and on arrival he was quickly solicited for his knowledge of the Ruhr. For a while he had a regular income selling his knowledge to the Americans, who were not yet in the war, and the English, who were. When the pace of the war increased, his intrinsic steel knowledge became of more use to the Japanese at home than in Sweden, and he was employed in a remote section of the Japanese Ministry of Information, a section, however, with importance infinitely greater than its size. The end of the war saw the end of the Japanese home steel production, and almost the end of Japan. Kotaro had extensive funds still hidden away in Switzerland and in Sweden, and promptly returned to Europe to claim them.

A resurgent Japan fifteen years after the end of the war gave him the opportunity he sought. He returned to Tokyo. The Olympic Games ended – and fortunately the sport at which he personally excelled was not on the official programme – Kotaro went to see the higher management of the resurgent Mitziguchi steel works. It took less than a week to establish his special department.

When the North American operator came on the line, Kotaro himself set up the television screen on to which the telephone call was played. The reproduction of each page was brilliant. Each page was photographed separately by polaroid mechanism and the prints were on his desk within minutes of the end of the call. He went through the 'Entry Forbidden' door and carried the papers down to the Bessemer platform. Mitziguchi had five blowers, compared with the four of International Steel Consortium. Mitziguchi had been working on a P-less steel for two years without success until an ever-open ear heard rumours of this new development in a call from the English steel works to the Head Office of Instecon in Zürich. The pages of the notebook were given to the Japanese Steel Manager. He read them faultlessly, and then issued his instructions. A meeting was called in half an hour's time, for all department heads from the blast furnace manager – the iron maker, the coke oven manager, the Bessemer managers, the steel maker. The ore purchasing agent was there, the chief metallurgist, the chief chemist. The managers of the rolling mills, the strip mills, the sheet mills, all were there. When the meeting ended after only twenty minutes, each knew that within two weeks Mitziguchi would be in the market with a phosphorus-free steel.

Phosphorus-free steel – the dream of steel and iron makers since the early days of puddled furnaces. Steel is a complex of iron and carbon, with other elements present in small amounts – oxygen, silicon, vanadium, manganese, sulphur, nitrogen, and most insidious of all, phosphorus. All the other elements improve the quality of the steel for a specific purpose, but even the slightest trace of phosphorus, as low as one part in one hundred thousand parts of steel, can destroy that ultimate ductility and tensile strength of which the scientists know steel to be capable. Phosphorus-free steel has been made in the crucible, laboriously constituted from its elements. But that process could not be simulated in the coarser vessel of the vast Bessemer blower. At least, not until Instecon had invented a means of scouring the liquid molten steel by chemical and mechanical means free of its inherent phosphorus traces. It had cost Instecon an investment of well over four million pounds to perfect the process, one of the best-kept secrets of the modern industrial world, comparable to the discovery of polythene, penicillin, and radar.

'K in England has done a good job,' said Kotaro Hitohori. The message was quickly conveyed.

# PHASE 2

Mrs Brannigan waited until half past three before making any inquiry about her husband, Evan. There was always the chance he was working late on the shift. With this new secret process they were all talking about, working hours of the steel-making crews had been unpredictable, and many's the good meal ruined waiting for Evan to climb the hill from the valley back home. And then there was the chance that after his shift he had called into the pub. Steel making was a dry process and nothing short of a gallon of good honest beer would usually serve the men when they had finished work. But, drunk or sober, she had never known Evan Brannigan not to get home after the pubs had closed. Always ravenously hungry with the beer inside him and powerfully sleepy, he would stagger home to a plate of food and an hour in the chair, come what may. When he didn't arrive home she walked down the road into the pub.

'Haven't seen Evan, have you?'

'Not today.'

From the Working Men's Club in the valley she toured every single pub on the route from the steel-making plant to his home on the hills above. Only when she learned that Evan had been seen in none did she begin to worry. Finally she presented herself at the gatehouse. Since Instecon took over from the family firm which formerly had owned the iron works it was forbidden for the gate-keeper to pass messages of a personal nature through to the inside of the plant. However, since the overtime worked in the Bessemer had increased, many were the calls at the gatehouse to verify the men were working and not, as might be expected, enjoying themselves in some nocturnal and secret perambulation.

'Evan Brannigan still on duty up there with you, then?' the gate-man asked the Bessemer plant office on the internal telephone, but no one could remember having seen Evan since the end of the night shift, since they had blown the last charge in Number 3. And there the matter rested for the rest of the day. Oddly enough, no one thought to look at the time sheet delivered at the end of the day to ascertain at what time Evan Brannigan had clocked off.

# PHASE 3

Though the Republic started producing its own iron ore from the iron mines of Serro in 1945 for the integrated steel plant at San Gabriel on the Pequena river forty miles south of Rosario, sufficient steel of a high quality is not yet being produced in the plant for the Republic to be self-supporting. Many hundreds of thousands of tons of steel are annually imported from the United States of America, England, and the continent of Europe. Much of this imported steel passes through the hands of Don José de Perrera, the principal purchasing officer for the Sociedad de Urbanización – the Development Corporation. A very important man, Señor Don José sees no one except by appointment. One morning a month after the inconsequential affair in the British plant of the International Steel Consortium, Don José saw two steel men. The second, William Brown, was late for his appointment. For weeks he had been trying to get into the Sociedad, for weeks he had failed. The previous week-end an E-type Jaguar was delivered at the port and was now parked outside a house on the outskirts of Avellencito. A telephone call was made from Avellencito to Rosario and on the receipt of it Señor Don José agreed to see Mr William Brown.

Mr William Brown was late. It was a hot day with the high humidity that seems to blow across the Cuchilla Grande all the way from Uruguay, a heavy sticky humidity that brings the surface of the River Plate with it. William Brown walked up the many stairs of the Sociedad and presented his card to the doorman. The doorman looked at it and waved William Brown on to a bench. He picked up the long-handled telephone and rang it. He stood to attention and spoke hesitantly into the instrument. After a while he seemed to be bowing from the waist. He put down the telephone and snapped his fingers. A boy dressed in a bright green uniform two sizes too big for him came running across the entrance hall. The doorman spoke to him in rapid Spanish. The boy nodded his head over and over again and then smiled a naïve smile at William Brown. He then walked before him across the entrance hall, up another flight of marble stairs and across a small hall. At the far end of the hall was a heavy mahogany iron-studded door. He knocked on the door and opened it. Inside was a male secretary. He dismissed the boy with a perfunctory wave of his hand and took William Brown across the carpet to another door. He rapped on the door, opened it and at long last William Brown was in the presence of Señor Don José de Perrera himself.

Señor Don José waved his secretary out. Mr Brown seated himself and Señor Don José offered him a cigar from the leather-covered humidor on his desk. He himself did not smoke but waited courteously until Mr Brown had lit his cigar.

'You know, Señor Brown, that we propose to build a bridge over the river at Verdades to connect with the town of Donasterio. This bridge will be made of steel, of course, and we anticipate requiring a considerable amount. Because of the nature of this bridge a special quality of steel will be required. I have been most impressed with the report which our technical people have prepared as a result of studying the specification of the steel which you are offering. However, in your specification you claim this steel to be the unique

28

invention of the company you represent, the International Steel Consortium of Zürich, etc. However . . .'

William Brown, familiar with the circuitous method of doing business in South America, was somewhat surprised at the direct statement. Señor Don José, what is more, had on his face a look that William Brown had only seen once before, on the face of a man who held a wild ace in a game of solo whist. Salesman that he was, he wondered what was about to come, and in advance he knew he was not going to enjoy it.

'However,' said Señor Don José, 'I find this statement not to be true, and I am therefore led to presume that perhaps other statements of yours may not be true, statements about quantities, and deliveries, and guarantees.'

Though William Brown was worried he showed no sign, too old a hand in the markets of the world to concede an advantage to a client. 'I should be most obliged, Señor Don José, if you could tell me in which way my statement is not true. I can only assume that the falsehood you allege is contained in a typographical error.' Try that one for size, you lucky bastard, he thought in language to which he was more accustomed.

Señor Don José was grinning hugely. He knew that, to use an American expression, he had William Brown over a barrel. 'It is not true,' he said, 'that you are the sole inventors of this special steel for which we had high hopes and which incidentally has made our style of architecture for this bridge to be possible. I have had an excellent meeting in my office this morning with a gentleman who, sitting in that very chair, informed me that he is able to offer steel of an analysis which appears on the face of it to be exactly similar to that of your steel, but at a cheaper price. To be brief, Mr Brown, your steel is neither unique nor inexpensive.'

William Brown could not believe his ears. Another steel with the same analysis as P-less, at a cheaper price? Zürich and London must be off their heads. He raged with the kind of fury a field representative can have for the Head Office. Didn't the bloody fools realize that, following the last sales briefing in Zürich, he had gone to town with P-less? Didn't they realize that he was out on a limb here in South America and that once he was caught out in this kind of mistake his name and the name of their Company would be gone? The Company should have checked it was unique.

Without speaking, Señor Don José reached into his desk drawer and took out a piece of steel bar, two inches long, one inch in diameter. He put it on the desk. 'The thing which most impressed us about your steel,' he said, 'was the high tensile strength and ductility, which my technical report tells me came from the total absence of phosphorus. This steel which I am offered today at only a fraction of the price of your steel is also said to be free of phosphorus. I shall send it later in the day to our government laboratories for analysis, but I have every confidence that the claims which have been made for it will be justified. In these circumstances I regret that you and I cannot do business together.'

'Can I have the steel?' William said hurriedly.

Señor Don José shook his head. 'I require it for analysis,' he said. 'But if you care to have a sample of it I am sure that the makers would supply one!'

'Who are they?' William asked.

'Mitziguchi Steel Works, Tokyo, Japan!'

# PHASE 4

The private plane touched down at Cardiff Airport, and Alec was whisked through Customs into a Company helicopter which set him down actually inside the gates on the lawns of what in the old ironmasters' day had been the family house. For four generations the Jones family had made steel here in the valleys. Computers looked at the lucrative possibilities in the valley through passionate but electronic eyes and click, click, clicked approval. And the valley became a tiny tooth in the vast maw of the International Steel Consortium. Where once the ironmaster had strode with a gun, helicopters landed and took off again and all manner of strange voices were heard. Workmen who had survived starvation, lost their virile identity, but had not sense to count the cost.

Alec Haig was an Englishman who swam against the tide. Adept at languages from a varied education at Oxford, the Sorbonne, Göttingen, he topped it all at Harvard with a Modern Business course. Then he returned to Europe to seek employment. Objective – top management. Basic Science – Oxford and Göttingen, Economics – Oxford and the Sorbonne, the Law – Göttingen and the Sorbonne. He wanted to be the president of a company, the managing director, the top spelaeologist in the vast vaulted caverns of power. He could have been a scientist, a barrister, an economist. He became a policeman, the one man in International Steel Consortium who knew enough about everything to discern any departure from pattern, any break with normality, any interruption in that even rhythm which is the outward and audible sign of master planning. International Steel was based on master planning. Thus, when the Swedish ore master was diluting the charge into the blast furnace to line his own pockets, it was Alec Haig who read the blast furnace analyses and the ore-charging specifications and perceived that someone was departing from a tradition. Gunnar Beglof sold whole train-loads of best Swedish ore, replaced them with inferior oxide, and pocketed the difference. Unfortunately for Gunnar Beglof, the inferior ore contained a trace, no more, of zirconium. Alec Haig knew the only source of zirconium was the low-grade ore mined at Plaslo, where Instecon did no business. At least, not officially. It was Alec Haig who read other reports from Instecon, Lyons, and knew the magic eye rejected inferior steel sheets on an average throughout the world of only 6·2 per cent. The rejected steel sheets were sold locally for scrap. The manager of the plant in Lyons had adjusted the magic eye to reject a proportion of sheets not inferior. These had been sold as scrap to a company of which a relation of the manager was a nominal shareholder. Pierre Lachasse was astounded when Alec Haig, after two visits only to Lyons, emptied and locked the sheet cutting shed and himself uncovered the distorted setting of the magic eye. Pierre Lachasse was lucky. He died of a cerebral haemorrhage when Alec Haig showed his findings.

Bill Brown's call from the Republic was received in Zürich at 5.30 a.m. Alec was on the private Instecon jet, a converted VC10, at 6.15 a.m. He arrived in Instecon, South Wales, at 7.30 a.m. A security office had been established by 10 a.m. containing a direct radio link to Zürich. A management committee meeting called for 10.15 a.m. started at 10.16 a.m. By 11 a.m. Alec Haig knew all details of steel production modifications since his last visit two years earlier. He started his tour of the plant, some three miles in length and over two miles wide, at 11.01 a.m., and by 12 noon was back in the Security office, on the telephone to Zürich.

Alec Haig was six feet one in height, weighed thirteen stone. His stomach was as flat as a board, his muscles hardened by constant exercise. During the war he fought with the Long Range Desert Group, with Popski's Private Army, and then with the Glider Pilot Regiment. He left the army in 1945 with an M.M. and bar and an M.C. and bar. He had the alertness of a trained athlete, the self-possession of a brigadier. Once he had been married, but his wife died tragically, and no one who knew him ever talked about her. He was sitting alone in the Security office at the conclusion of his radio talk with Zürich. Maximum security had been imposed on South Wales like a steel curtain.

Alec was reading reports, from every department in the plant, hastily compiled since his arrival. As usual he was looking for anomalies, curious incidents, odd snippets and fragments of information. He doubted he would find what he was looking for in the reports – such fragmentary information usually came to him in an off-guarded conversation, a sentence that begins 'funny thing happened yesterday', or 'I don't suppose it matters but . . .'. Alec had trained himself to elicit such comments without anyone being aware, other than himself, that they had been said.

'Coke oven needs looking at,' he said to himself, the information automatically filed for early action. The chemists' analysis of the coking process revealed a high sulphur content on what Alec could discern was a pattern. It looked as if one of the three shifts of coke masters was inefficient. Or malcontent, a possible potential saboteur. A man who leaves too much sulphur when he's burning coal into coke either

33

doesn't know his job – and all specialists employed by ISC knew their jobs – or he isn't trying. This could be accidental or deliberate. It might be personal – wife playing around, short of money, kid failed an important exam, in which case Personnel had a mechanical procedure for helping, or it could be deliberate, part of a chain in a process of impending production, of reducing the quality of the product. Give me four malcontents in any factory, Alec always said, and I can stop production overnight, or worse still, I can so reduce quality that no one will buy.

Alec had been reading for three hours, with additional reports being brought to him at intervals, when he got his first twinge, his first feeling that something was wrong. He was reading a report concerned with day-to-day finance. He picked up the telephone, consulted the local dial card and dialled a number. 'This item in the suspense account that appears to be transferred from the wages account. What is it?'

'Odd thing, that. One of the men on the Bessemer didn't collect his pay. Name, if I remember correctly, is Brannigan. Since he didn't clock off at the end of his last shift . . .'

'Didn't clock off?'

'That's right. He left the factory without clocking off. Most odd, that. He'll lose money by it!'

It took the Personnel office only a few minutes to bring over the Employees file on Evan Brannigan, with a report about the visits made by Mrs Brannigan. Alec immediately sent a car to her house. She was flustered when she arrived – car riding was something she did not often do.

'*I* don't think he left the works,' she said. There, it was out in the open, the terrible fear that had haunted her since she realized that Evan was not coming home. She didn't believe all the sly remarks that Evan had run away with another woman. You can tell if somebody else is feeding your cat, can't you, by his appetite at home. But, to suggest her husband might still be inside the factory, when Personnel had told her he had left the factory without clocking off, well, that was something she couldn't bring herself to do.

They searched the entire plant, starting with the Bessemers and spreading out from there to cover each of the other departments. No trace could they find.

'I want to know everything Evan Brannigan does in the course of his working day,' Alec said to the Bessemer manager. 'Every single thing.'

'We've got two loads to blow on this shift, you know.' The Bessemer manager was truculent. The man would turn up again – they always did – with a cock-and-bull story about his grandmother's funeral or some such rubbish. One glance at the face of Alec Haig convinced him that you did what this man asked, instantly. Slowly, meticulously they reconstructed one day in the life of Evan Brannigan. It was the assistant manager who ended the sequence. 'I stand at these dials watching the blowing, and then, when the blowing has finished, I give my clipboard to Brannigan, and he takes it into the office here' – they walked across to the office together – 'and I imagine he puts it down on the table and then either goes off shift or goes to the canteen to get a cup.'

'And these notes on this clipboard – you've never missed any?'

'Never.'

'What are they?'

'They're the progress of the blow. Copies of the notes we keep in these files. I just take one copy out to check against the actual blowing.'

'What exactly?'

'Composition of the metal, temperature, the time of each

35

blow, various readings for the composition of the gas as it comes out of the metal. Chemical formulae, quantities. Oxygen pressure and composition going in, things like that, you know.'

'If I had your notes in Lyons, for example, I could get steel of exactly the same composition?'

The Bessemer manager looked puzzled. It was the Zürich office that had appointed him, to try to get a uniform system that could be applied to all the steel-producing plants of the International Steel Consortium. 'Yes, if you had my notes!'

Alec looked grave. 'So anyone who has those notes can blow phosphorus-free steel any time!'

# PHASE 5

'You never know, but I just thought there might be something in this!' The chief chemist was apologetic as he put on Alec Haig's table a sheaf of papers and a sample of metal about the size of a cricket ball.

Alec started to read – the papers were headed 'Batch Sample Analysis number 10027', dated the previous day. On the mimeographed form figures had been pencilled in as each of the laboratory technicians completed his part of the routine analysis. Alec noted the sample date and time – the metal had been taken from the last Bessemer load blown on Brannigan's shift. His eye ran down the column of figures. He noted in passing the tiny proportion of phosphorus. The report had been signed by the chief chemist – that is to say the chief chemist had started to sign it and then, like Alec Haig, his attention had been drawn back up the page by the one anomaly, the one figure that, to a trained eye, stood out like Cleopatra's needle.

'That figure for the calcium content, and the trace of phosphorus!'

'It's right. Checked it myself.' The chief chemist looked at Alec Haig in admiration; only an expert could have spotted the curious entry.

'The calcium content is too high. About one hundred times too high. And I thought the batch was P-less!'

'So it was – at the Bessemer. But somewhere between the

Bessemer and the sample bay that steel became adulterated by a large amount of calcium.'

'And a small amount of phosphorus.'

Alec Haig picked up the personnel files and extracted the personal details of Evan Brannigan. He pulled a scratch pad in front of him and made a quick calculation. The chief chemist watched him.

'Can you give me an average figure for calcium content?'

'Call it three noughts five, plus or minus one.'

Alec made a note on the pad. From his pocket he took a miniaturized transistored calculator. Within seconds he looked up at the chief chemist, who drew from his pocket a piece of paper on which he had written a calculation before their meeting.

'I assumed Brannigan weighed twelve stone,' he said, as he put his calculation on the table, 'and my calculation gave a calcium reading slightly low. I would say Brannigan, from these figures, weighed thirteen stone.'

'He weighed fifteen,' Alec said, sombrely. 'But a lot of that was the belly of a heavy beer drinker, not calciferous bone.'

'He must have slipped and fallen into the vat?'

'He must have!'

Alec knew Brannigan couldn't have fallen into the vat of molten steel. The railway line ran at least nine feet clear of the Bessemer rails. Brannigan couldn't even have jumped as far as the vat, no matter how strong the fear that had motivated him. No, Brannigan had been picked up, and thrown. And that made it murder!

'What kind of man murders another man to gain secret knowledge of an industrial process?' Alec thought, though he concealed his deep revulsion from the chief chemist, who went from the office sorrowfully shaking his head. How much more sorrowful he would have been had he known the true nature of Brannigan's ending. Lust for power, greed, envy, fear, these are the motives that cause men to kill, to strike the spark of life from a fellow human. Alec had met them all during the war, so long ago, and still was appalled to meet them again in peace. Industrial espionage was a game to him most of the time – granted it was played for high stakes and therefore had a steel-cored set of rules. But normally, the price of failure was business ruin, or the heavy loss of money, and the spies themselves, the pawns on the international board, were rarely brought into personal combat, seldom saw their enemies face to face except smiling over a cocktail glass.

'There will be tears for you, Evan Brannigan, and mine were nothing, had I such to give ... !' He thought of the widow, coming to the gate, convinced that, in some mysterious way, her life and the life of Evan Brannigan had split apart; and though he had never met her husband except through the reports of his men, Alec felt an intolerable compassion for her. You pay a man to do certain work for you, you demand his abilities be extended in your service, and his loyalties. You take a small part of him, and you buy it, demanding he exert himself on your behalf. But how can you ask him to die for you?

Alec himself went to Mrs Brannigan's house. A Company car dropped him at the end of her street, and he walked down. He wanted to arrive unannounced, to see for himself the kind of home Brannigan and twenty years of hard work had established. He hadn't been in the front parlour five minutes before he knew that, if Brannigan had any loose money at his disposal, bribery money for example, he spent none of it on his home.

'Go out much, your husband?'

'Not much. A few pints of beer at the club or the pub, and back home again by nine o'clock, that was Evan. If he wasn't working it was home every night and in bed by ten o'clock.' Mrs Brannigan did not cry when he told her the news, and all she could find to say when he told her she would be compensated by the Company was, 'Very grateful, I'm sure, very grateful.'

Alec knew what the loss of her husband would mean to the widow – the arid life to which his death would inevitably condemn her.

'I wonder if there is just a small request I might make,' Mrs Brannigan was saying to him. 'You said they had a sample of the steel and that's how they found it all out?'

'That's right,' Alec said.

'I wonder – if it wouldn't be a bother and put you to any expense – do you think I might possibly have that sample? After all, it's what you might call his last mortal remains on earth, isn't it?'

Alec dismissed the car and walked back to the plant through the mean streets. At times like this, he almost hated his job.

# PHASE 6

'I don't like it, gentlemen, I don't like it one little bit. Certainly we have had our troubles here in South Wales but I can assure you we've never had anything such as this. Workmen jumping or thrown into vats of molten steel! We have a very high record of industrial safety here in South Wales, and I don't like it.'

'He's at it again,' Sodaberg's gaze seemed to say to Alec Haig, sitting opposite him across the boardroom table. An emergency meeting of the board had been called as soon as the facts about Brannigan had been uncovered. Sodaberg flew directly from Zürich that afternoon, arriving at the plant only twenty minutes before the start of the meeting.

'There's no point in beating about the bush. We've invented a new steel we hoped would keep this entire plant on full production for a long time to come. Now the Japanese have that secret – how, it's up to Alec to discover. At the present time our rolling capacity is well above our order book, and frankly, without the phosphorus-free contracts – and we don't look like getting any if the Japs undercut us – we shall have to consider mass redundancy. You're just not paying your way here, Mr Reynolds, and Instecon can't carry South Wales any longer. My purpose in coming here is to state our true position. You had ten minutes before the meeting to read it. With the loss of our advantage on P-less steel, we shall have to consider redundancies of at least 750 men throughout the plant – you will find a schedule of exactly which departments they are to come from in the appendix to the report.'

The Managing Director's complexion had turned from its usual ruddy red to a fierce purply blue. 'Redundancy!' he thundered. 'Redundancy? I won't hear the word. Why, I know personally every man who works at this plant!'

Sodaberg looked at him, no trace of emotion on his face. He knew Fletcher, a bread-and-butter director, would support him. In an arid voice, as if reading the cattle auction prices he said, 'I propose a motion to this meeting that Mr Reynolds be asked to resign as Managing Director of this Company. My reasons for proposing this motion,' he continued, equally drily, 'are that the majority does not think it is in the best interests of the Company to have Mr Reynolds continue in his capacity as Managing Director.'

The Old Man rose, and with a dignity none could deny, he walked across the boardroom, opened the door and went out. There was a silence.

'I'll take over as Managing Director,' Sodaberg said.

'He's right, you know,' Alec said quietly.

'Who's right?'

'The Old Man. This is no time for redundancy talks.'

'I am merely implementing the decisions of the retiring Managing Director,' Sodaberg said, a thin smile on his lips. 'They won't hold the redundancies against us.'

'You're a bastard, Sodaberg!'

'I don't understand what you mean,' Sodaberg blustered. 'I've been sent here from Central Management to keep this place running as effectively as possible; it won't help if I get sentimental about the feelings of a dispensable Managing Director. The Company . . .'

Alec Haig looked at him in disgust. 'Some men who work

42

for a big company such as ours respect it for what it is, a collection of the best available talents determined to work with other men as humanely as possible. Other men use the Company to crush all resistance, all decency of feeling. Those men invariably bring the Company into disrepute. That's the kind of bastard you are, Sodaberg, a Company bastard.'

Sodaberg looked as though he wanted to hit him, but Alec smiled blandly. 'I'll talk to Zürich about that,' he said, his face flushed with anger.

'You do that,' Alec said. 'You talk to the Head of Central Management in Zürich, and when you've finished, ask the switchboard to connect me with the Chairman, because that's who I'll be talking to. Don't let my official title of Head of Technical Sales, Miscellaneous, fool you. That word Miscellaneous covers a lot of things you know nothing about, including direct speech with the Chairman, who doesn't like bastards using the Company any more than I do.'

# PHASE 7

'You'd better make that last!' Frank Lester said, as he put on his trousers.

Pamela stirred in the bed, warm, comfortable, sated. 'I like it better when you come in the mornings,' she said. 'Apart from anything else, I get a cup of tea in bed!'

'And that's not all you get!' Frank said jokingly.

Pamela didn't answer. Frank Lester worked in the coke ovens. As far as his wife knew, over at Cymbran, he did a ten-hour shift. She would have raised blue bloody murder, he thought, if she knew where he spent the first two hours of his shift! Luckily Pamela, married young and widowed almost immediately in the Cyprus campaign, lived in a house near the gates, with a most convenient back door through which he could slide in or out, with no one the wiser.

'Yes, you'll have to make that last,' he repeated. 'This is my last night shift on the coke ovens. I've been moved.'

What he was saying finally penetrated Pamela's torpor. 'Where're you being moved to, then?'

'Up to the top of the slag dump. Driving a shovel.'

'Why've they shifted you from the coke ovens? You been misbehaving or something?'

'Not me! They've moved all our team, every single one. They sacked the team leader on the spot this morning. There'll be a row about it in the unions, I can tell you. But as far as we're concerned, it'll mean no more trips down here at the start of the shift to see you.'

Pamela pouted. 'You'll have to arrange some other time then, won't you? Unless you're getting bored with me!'

He walked back across to the bed and kissed her roughly on the mouth. 'Does that feel as if I'm getting bored?'

She pulled him to her again. 'If you'd told me this was going to be the last time, we could have stayed in bed a bit longer!'

'Yes, and be late for work, I suppose.'

As usual, Alec Haig had acted ruthlessly and quickly.

# PHASE 8

David Davies, the coke oven foreman, walked across the factory site towards the ovens, stretched in a long row at the end of the roadway from the blast furnace.

'Dai's early tonight!' he thought. He could see the short stocky figure on the flat roof of the ovens, sweeping the coal dust spread by the charging chutes. Down by the gas line, Eddy Newman was tidying up before going off shift. It would be a long night, David knew, a long crisp night. Might even be a bit of rain before morning, and the chrysanthemums could certainly do with that. He had his eye on a couple of plants at the back of his garden, where they caught the winter sun by the privet hedge. If all went well, he'd be showing those over at Cymbran. That was his last living thought.

An explosion starts from nothing. A man opens a valve, thinking there is no gas in the line. But he's mistaken. There's a flash. The flash itself is insignificant. The pressure builds up inside, until it gets too much to be contained. The bricks start to fly. 'My God, it's going up!' were the last words David Davies spoke before a brick from the rear wall of the coke oven hit him on the chin and carried away most of his head. A current of high speed air whipped round the side of the oven and wrapped Eddy Newman round the pipe work, the secondary blast ripped him through the pipes like meat through a sausage machine. Dai went up into the air straight from the roof of the furnace, and then the roof itself came up in the air to meet him coming down, and pounded him to small pieces. The whole coke oven bay exploded. Within seconds the ground was cleared of all bricks, machinery, coal, and glowing coke. The charging crane buckled and fell over, a mass of twisted strands like dropped knitting. The railway engine that carried the glowing coke to the quenching was propelled along the railway lines and crashed into the water tower. The water tank itself buckled at the knees and tipped ten thousand gallons of water on to the flaming rails and the side of the ore grading shed. Only then did the noise come, the whiplash crack of the actual explosion, the rumble as the ovens gathered pressure, and the almighty expiration when brickwork gave way and bricks smashed into the air like missiles. The debris rose high, came pouring down again, brick upon brick upon steel plates, until the whole area sounded with the clashing clamour of a regiment of demoniacally thrashed giant kettledrums. The valve which controlled the coal gas flow was flung against the steel girders of the ore grading shed, splattering the bronze metal like so much cake dough. No one would ever see it had been left in the danger position, the safety lock deliberately hinged back against all regulations. Joe Michaels from the steel sheet packing plant was already at home when the explosion occurred.

# PHASE 9

Antonio Giovanni took the key to room four-six-eight from the clerk behind the desk of the Hotel Dos Riojas Santas, in Punta de l'Este, Uruguay. He went up in the lift, along the corridor to his room which overlooked the ocean, took off his white shirt and put on a black roll-neck sweater of thin cashmere. The time was ten o'clock.

Ten minutes earlier, in the elegant dining-room which also overlooked the ocean, he had watched the arrival of the Japanese salesman with a tall blonde Nordic girl. They crossed to a table beneath a striped umbrella, on the balcony poised above the water. Señor Atahualpa Vizcaya rose from his seat and greeted them. The Japanese salesman presented his tall blonde companion. Atahualpa's eyes came to life as he held her hand and kissed it. She would be a diversion from what had promised to be a tedious dinner, discussing steel supplies. 'Sit here, beside me,' he said, 'where you can look out over the ocean.'

She smiled, and seated herself gracefully on the chair the Japanese was holding for her. Atahualpa took the menu from the hovering waiter. 'Now, what shall we order?' he asked. He seemed already to have forgotten the smiling little man, whose informant on Atahualpa's tastes had not been mistaken.

Giovanni crossed to the terrace window of his room, opened it and stepped out. He walked to the edge and glanced

48

on to the balcony of the adjoining suite. The window into the sitting-room was open. Silently he leapt over the wall separating the two balconies. The sitting-room was empty. He went inside. On a desk stood the bulky briefcase of the Japanese salesman. It was locked. Giovanni took a key from his pocket and opened the briefcase. Inside were a number of papers he ignored. At the bottom, however, in the centre compartment, was a small wooden box. He opened it. It contained a metal bar, three inches long, an inch in diameter. He took the bar out of the box and went back to his own room the way he had come. He picked up the telephone and rapidly placed a call. Then he settled down to wait. Thirty minutes later there came a knock on his door. He opened it. A thin-faced, nervous young man waited there, came rapidly into the room and from his pocket produced a metal bar identical in size and shape to the one Giovanni had taken from the bag of the Japanese salesman.

'What's in it?' Giovanni asked.

'All sorts of rubbish!'

'Phosphorus?'

'Enough to start a fire.'

Giovanni took the metal bar, crossed the wall between the two balconies and placed the bar in the bottom of the Japanese salesman's briefcase. Then he locked the briefcase and returned to his own room. The young man had already left.

'Wait until Vizcaya's analysts get hold of that!' he said. 'They won't buy as much as a collar stud from the Japanese!'


Giovanni was almost asleep when he heard the laughter from the next suite, Atahualpa's deep booming voice dominating the sound. The dinner had obviously been a good one, with enough wine to make a show of removing inhibitions. Giovanni smiled to himself, turned over and went to sleep. The Japanese salesman was sitting on the sofa in the suite. Atahualpa and the girl were both seated together, he on the arm of her chair. His hand was draped casually about her shoulders, his fingers inserted beneath the shoulder strap of her dress. He bent his head down to whisper into her ear.

The girl glanced across at the Japanese salesman. With an almost imperceptible nod he indicated the bedroom door. She rose from her chair and went across and into the bedroom, one of two the suite possessed. Atahualpa watched her walk across the room.

'I like your secretary,' he said. 'How long will she stay in Punta de l'Este?'

'Why don't you go and ask her?' the Japanese salesman replied, his face bland and inscrutable.

Atahualpa looked across at him, his eyes narrowed. 'No cameras?' he asked.

The Japanese shook his head. 'No tape recorders either,' he added.

Atahualpa walked across to the door and, with an innate sense of delicacy, he knocked.

'Just a minute,' the voice came from within. Then, a couple of minutes later, 'You can come in,' she said.

The Japanese salesman watched the door close behind Atahualpa, then sighed with relief. For a moment it had been touch and go, but he knew he could rely on Mina to leave her handbag on the bedside cabinet, the glass handle pointing towards the bed. He took his briefcase, unlocked it and took out the folder of papers, preparing for a few hours' work. But then the position of the box containing the metal sample caught his eye. He took the box from the bag, using his handkerchief to grip it, and gently took off the lid. He breathed a sigh of relief when he saw the sample still there. He took the sample out of the bag and upended it.

The wrong Japanese number had been stamped on it.

# PHASE 10

Alec Haig himself went to Customs at London Airport to collect the parcel from Giovanni in Uruguay. It was in an ordinary brown paper envelope, in an ordinary cardboard box, stamped, 'Sample: to await collection at London Airport'. In his hand he held the telegram notifying the flight and the waybill number. The plane had been on the ground for an hour when the freight was brought through into the Customs shed. Though chafing at the delay, he showed no signs of impatience. He received the sample from the Customs officer, opened the parcel for inspection, and had left the Customs shed behind in five minutes. The traffic was light as he turned the DB6 into the westbound stream. Though they kept a fully staffed laboratory at the Gower Street, London, headquarters of Instecon, for security reasons he preferred to take the sample down to South Wales for analysis. He made good time to Chepstow, not even stopping for a drink on the way. From Chepstow he took the B4235 in the direction of Usk. The time was about half-past five, and dusk had begun to descend. Soon it would be dark. As he passed the Shire Newton crossroads, an Alfa Romeo pulled out of the side road and turned along the road to Usk. Alec braked hard, cursing careless drivers, especially women. He could see the flash of light-coloured hair as the Alfa gathered speed just in front of him. He flicked his headlights once as a signal. The girl driver touched her sidelights but drove straight on in front of him. They raced along the road one after the other, as they entered the trees of Went Wood. Here the light faded rapidly and both switched on headlights. Alec kept his dipped out of courtesy. That the girl was a first-class driver became apparent with each bend in the road, since she rarely dropped her speed more than ten miles an hour to take them. Each time she drove with an immaculate precision, never cutting the corner, never edging nearer the side. Alec found himself admiring her driving more and more, resolved to keep up with her. They were dropping down the hill past Earlswood Common when suddenly he noticed her cutting in to the inside of a right-angle bend.

'Silly woman,' he muttered. 'If anyone was coming round that bend she wouldn't stand a chance.'

He stayed on the left side of the road as she cut the corner almost completely on the right side of the road. Both cars were doing a good eighty miles an hour. As she got into the bend, she flicked on the reversing light, and the beam suddenly cut back at him, dazzling him completely. Through the light haloes he saw the bulk of a lorry parked on his side of the road. He wrenched the wheel to the right to try to follow her past it, but the reversing light on the Alfa Romeo dazzled him. He pulled the wheel savagely to the left and yanked on the handbrake. The back end of the DB6 slewed round, until his bonnet was headed for the ditch. He snapped off the handbrake, and pressed down hard on the accelerator. The DB6 shot forward into the ditch on the side of the road, between the parked lorry and the hedge. He felt the DB6 tilt over to the left, but kept his foot down. The car scraped along the side of the lorry, with an ear-rending shriek of torn metal, but then it cleared the back of the lorry and he was able to pull the wheel to the right back on to the hard surface. The girl had stopped the Alfa Romeo on the side of the road, and had opened her door and was about to get out. Unable to correct his steering in time, Alec rammed the front of the DB6 into the back panel of the Alfa. The girl screamed as the car smashed forward into her. The car bucked forward, and the DB6 was clear. Without hesitation, Alec put down his foot again and the DB6 leaped forward. He hadn't gone fifty yards down the road before he heard the whang of a bullet against the back bumper. The second bullet shattered the back window, and then he was around the next corner out of range, the screams of the golden-haired girl still ringing in his ears.

# PHASE II

'Who handled that telex machine?' Alec asked. He was furious, and didn't care who knew it. The encounter on the road had shaken him more than he cared to say.

'It's the A wire,' Sally said, 'and only Mr Sodaberg and I saw the message and the waybill number.'

Alec looked hard at her. She had been the private secretary to Samuel Reynolds for three years. Her record was impeccable. A local-born girl, she had never left the country except to go to the Costa Brava for her annual holiday. Joe Michaels, her father, worked in the steel sheet packing plant. She'd taken shorthand and typing in the local school, and had worked her way up through the typists, pool, the Accounts office, secretary and then private secretary to the Old Man himself. A gorgeous girl of twenty-eight, she had never married. Tall, with a full figure, there were few men in and around the steel town who could deserve her, and well she knew it.

'Somebody knew we were expecting a shipment, and in plenty of time to lie in wait for me.' It rankled with him that he had been caught in such an easy trap, chasing a pretty girl down a country lane.

'The telex came from Zürich on the private A wire. Possibly someone at that end knew about it?'

'It could be,' he said.

She came across and put her hand on his arm. 'Are you

sure you're all right?' she asked in her lilting Welsh voice. 'That car of yours is very badly smashed down one side.'

'I'm all right,' he said. 'But thanks for asking! There are many people round here wouldn't be sorry to see the last of me.'

'They don't understand,' she said. 'They think you've just come to close the works down. They don't realize that in your own way you're trying to keep jobs for them. I'll get you some tea.'

'A drink would be more appropriate!'

She smiled, her face friendly and understanding. 'I imagine it would be,' she said. 'I'll get you one while you see the chief chemist. Scotch and water?'

'Large scotch, small water!'

The chief chemist looked surprised as he presented his report. 'This is exactly like our steel,' he said, 'but it doesn't conform in points of detail to any batch we've produced. Except one, very important factor . . .'

'No phosphorus, eh?'

'That's right. Not a trace. And one other thing. It doesn't have a batch number stamped on it, like all our samples. It's got these strange squiggles, like Chinese writing!'

---

Kotaro Hitohori heard of the explosion in the coke oven by a devious route – as was to be expected. The first hint of anything wrong in the South Wales factory came from the early warning of a future delay in a steel order for a bridge in Jamaica. The appropriate radio section monitored an exchange of bitter telegrams between the South Wales factory, the agent in Jamaica, and the Montego Bay Construction Company. The second hint came from an exchange of telex messages between the British Instecon Insurance Company, which handled the South Wales Instecon account, and an American subsidiary with whom they frequently underwrote large risks. After the so-called accident, Joe Michaels stayed away from work for a few days, with a National Health doctor's certificate which stipulated vaguely, Nervous Disorder. The man in black had to wait until Joe Michaels showed his face before he could make contact with him, since he could not risk being seen going to the house. Finally, he stood beside the bar in the local pub, with Joe beside him. Not that you would have known the two men were together, after their initial casual greetings.

'Who did it, Joe?'

'Did what?'

'The coke oven?'

'Search me. Surely it was an accident!'

'Impossible – too many safety devices! Did you do it, Joe?'

'Nobody will ever prove it!'

'They won't like it!'

'I don't give a damn what they like. It's time we had some real action round here, instead of taking bits of pictures with a camera.'

The man in black's knuckles grew white around the half-pint mug of beer he was holding. Joe could see his face reflected in the glass behind the bar, between the spirits bottles on their optic measures. The man's face looked distorted by a fierce, passionate anger.

'How many times do I have to tell you, Joe, that independent action like that does nobody any good. The whole place is insured. With the money they'll get, they'll build a bigger and better, more modern coke works, and you'll have achieved precisely nothing.'

Joe was truculent, like a dog who knows he's done wrong, and waits in fearful anticipation for punishment. But Joe was a man of action, and the cold slow world of industrial espionage meant nothing to him in his personal vendetta against the works. Before Instecon took over, Joe had been due for promotion to foreman. Another man had been given the job because the steel manager, appointed by Instecon, thought he had better qualities than Joe. That, and Joe's fierce feelings of Wales for the Welsh had been enough to make him ripe for recruitment into Kotaro's network. But, with his lack of discipline and his zeal for direct action, Joe was becoming difficult to control.

When the message reached Mitziguchi, Kotaro thought only for a moment, then made a flowing Japanese sign across the face of Joe's personal file, handed to him with the information about the coke oven. Translated, the Japanese sign would read: 'Eliminate'.

58

# PHASE 13

Though Samuel Reynolds was still packing when Alec Haig went to see him, his natural civility triumphed, and he invited Haig to take a drink. His son, Peter Reynolds, came into the sitting-room, in the house Samuel Reynolds and his wife occupied just inside the steel works perimeter. His animosity to Alec Haig was plain to see, but Alec took no heed.

'*Peter* Reynolds, isn't it? You work in the sheet steel sales department, if I remember correctly?' He put out his hand. Peter looked for a moment as if he would refuse, but the glint in his father's eye warned him, and he seized the proffered hand and shook it. He poured himself a drink from the sideboard, and asked to be excused. It was apparent he had no time to spare for the man he thought partly responsible for sacking his father. When he had gone, Samuel Reynolds took his drink and sat down in his chair by the fireplace, opposite Alec Haig.

'Wife and I are leaving on a world cruise next week,' he said. 'See all those places they write about in the newspapers!'

'Retirement would be hard for you?' Alec asked.

'Hard – it'll be damned impossible! Can you see me, taking the dogs for a walk, doing the *Telegraph* crossword! My family's men have always died in harness.'

'Perhaps you will,' Alec said.

'What do you mean?'

'I can't say any more at the moment,' Alec said.

'Can't say any more? You haven't said anything at all yet!'

'Can we leave it at this,' Alec urged. 'Will you postpone your cruise until after I get back from abroad?'

'I didn't know you were going abroad. When are you leaving?'

'I don't quite know yet.'

'It's a bit vague, isn't it?'

'In my job, Mr Reynolds,' Alec said, 'I've learned to live with vagueness.'

'Well, I haven't!' The old spirit was rising in Samuel Reynolds, the blunt, hard, direct man of iron who never used an 'if' or a 'but' or a 'maybe' in his life.

Alec was quick to change the subject. He knew the old man wouldn't leave on his cruise. Not yet, anyway. 'I want a good man,' he said, 'one of the workmen. He must be absolutely reliable, able to keep his mouth shut, Welsh, but not a supporter of the Free Society or any other nationalist organization, physically fit, and popular with the rest of the men. Any suggestions, since you know all the men personally?'

Samuel Reynolds thought for a brief moment. True to form he asked no questions. He chuckled. 'You had such a man as that,' he said, smiling, 'but you sent him away to exile on the top of the mountain. Frank Lester, from the coke oven. Up the hill driving a mechanical shovel and, I hear, like a wild cat because he can't get to see his girl-friend.'

'Frank Lester! Yes, I remember him. One of the crew who might have been sabotaging the coking!'

'Sabotage? Frank Lester? Never in a hundred years. He had a lovely widow woman just by the back gate – he'd be the last man to bother himself about sabotage. Anyway, he's not the man to go sneaking around blowing up his mates. Never in a hundred years!'

It was bitterly cold the following morning when Alec got out of his hired car at the top of the slag hill. He had taken the back route, by Brynfyn, so no one would see him. Frank Lester was already at work, driving the mechanical shovel, spreading out the loads of slag as they came tipping out of the buckets suspended from the endless wire that wound down the hill and part across the valley into the steel works below. From the top of the slag heap you could see the Beacons, and down through the valleys to the coastline twelve miles away. From the works came the rhythmic pounding of machinery, and the occasional plume of steam as they quenched one of the two coke ovens that had not been destroyed. Frank drove the shovel across towards the car and then jumped out. He was wrapped in a thick donkey jacket against the wind. Alec looked quickly around – no one was in sight of the two of them. Frank came across to warn him of trespassing, but then stopped when he recognized the man in the car. Alec opened the door.

'Get in,' he said. 'That's a knife-edged wind you have out there.'

'Get used to it, you do,' Frank said.

Alec came straight to the point. 'Mr Reynolds spoke very highly of you last evening,' he said.

'Much obliged, I'm sure,' Frank said, his Welshness heightened by embarrassment.

'What do you think of the Free Society?'

'I haven't thought much about it, to be honest.'

'But you must have some opinion?'

'Well, it's all a bit old-fashioned, really, isn't it? All this

61

nationalistic talk. I mean, the world's grown a bit too small to be talking about Wales for the Welsh, or England for the English, hasn't it?'

Ten minutes later they had achieved an understanding – Frank had a promise of ten pounds a week extra from the special fund, and would be returning to the coke ovens the following day.

'Never thought I'd be signing on as a spy,' Frank said, obviously delighted with the turn of events.

'You're not – you're a service of local information!'

Samuel Reynolds had chosen his man well, Alec thought, but would throw a fit if he knew the use Alec was making of him. As Frank got out of the car Alec called after him: 'One person I know will be delighted.'

Frank stopped and looked cautiously at him. 'Who would you have in mind?' he asked, warily.

'A certain widow woman, lives down by the back gate!'

Frank almost blushed. 'Didn't know as you were acquainted,' he said.

A cold hard look had come to Alec's face. 'Try not to forget it,' he said. 'I should hate to have to tell your wife.'

He let in the clutch of the car and drove out of the tipping area. Frank watched him go. 'Iron hand in the velvet glove, that one,' he said to himself. Now he knew why they were paying him ten pounds a week.

# PHASE 14

Dropping into Zürich Airport is the most pleasant landing possible. Alec always thought so, enjoyed the way the plane took only one run and circled round the side of the mountain, like a ball dropping against the edge of a bucket and spinning gently round. One moment the only sight was one of mountains. The next moment, the aeroplane tilted gracefully to the right, round the edge of a mountain top, and levelled out into the cup whose centre contained the ancient city of Zürich. Instecon's world headquarters was on the side of the lake, near the broadcasting station and the opera house, its existence advertised by the smallest of plaques, in unpolished bronze on the door that led to the street. Alec drove the Mercedes he always kept parked in Zürich Airport down the street past the Instecon headquarters and turned down towards the lake. Half-way down was a large gate on the right. He turned the car into it, the photo-electric cell on the front of the gate catching the beam from the small light he had switched on, low down on his car. The gate opened, silently, and he drove through into the large courtyard beyond. Only six cars were in the courtyard – only six had the necessary photo-electric equipment to open the gate. No windows of offices overlooked this courtyard, and few people knew of its existence. He got out of his car and walked to a metal door set in one wall. He opened the door with what seemed an ordinary business card. A metal pattern sealed into the pasteboard operated the electronic lock. The door was one side of a lift. He let the lift door close behind him, and used his card to bring the lift back up to the normal working level. As the doors opened at the ground floor, several members of staff got in.

'Had a nice trip, Mr Haig?' asked one girl, from the Sales department. Alec was nominally a member of the Technical Sales department.

'Not bad,' Alec said, 'but tiring.'

One of these days he must take that young lady out to dinner. She looked more than promising. They both disembarked at the top floor. She walked along the corridor in front of him, totally aware that he was inspecting her. Then, at the end of the corridor, she turned left into Sales, and he turned right into Technical Sales. He went through to his own office, to be greeted by Ilsa, his own secretary, a doughty lady hovering gracefully on this side of fifty. As soon as she saw him she began to flutter.

'Welcome home, Mr Haig,' she said. 'I've a hundred messages for you.' Mostly they were from Klaus Biedmacher, his Technical Sales assistant who, truth to tell, did all the selling in the department, and never knew how effectively he screened his boss. Alec went into his inner office and spent twenty minutes coping with the messages from Klaus. Then he shooed his secretary out with the injunction that on no account was he to be disturbed.

'*Ja*, rest and get some sleep after your tiring business trip,' she said.

As she went out he dropped the lock on the door. He picked up the internal telephone and dialled three numbers that didn't appear in the official inter-office telephone directory. The voice of his Managing Director answered.

'Right away?'

'In five minutes.'

Alec went to the sofa across one wall, sat on it beneath a landscape painting, and pressed a knob concealed in the leather behind the back. The whole wall, including the sofa, turned on its axis. On the other side the wall carried an identical picture, an identical sofa.

The office was smaller. In it a desk. Sitting behind the desk, his other secretary, Françoise, as different from Ilsa as it is possible to be.

'Hello!' she said, and stretched out her hands. He crossed the office quickly and enveloped her in his arms. When he stopped kissing her, both were breathless. 'Back soon,' he said, and stepped through the door at the far side of the office. This entire wing was sealed off from the rest of the Instecon office, its presence unknown to all but the men and the confidential secretaries who maintained them. Here were revealed the other faces of Instecon. Here the other directors' meetings were held, the strategy meetings, the meeting to plan the effective disposition of the approximate ten thousand million pound sterling equivalent empire these men controlled.

They were seated round the boardroom table, awaiting him. At the head of the table, Sir Barton Underwood, fourteenth baronet of a feudal line that went back to William the Conqueror. No effete grouse-shooting ride-to-hounds country squire was Sir Barton. His father had died at an early age, scarlet-faced, rotten with pheasant and port. Sir Barton, vegetarian, never drank. He had watched the servants carry the mouldering seventeen-stone hulk of his father up to the bedroom in Birton Hall, then went outside and sacked the gamekeeper and the groom. His father had been paying maintenance for thirteen bastards in and around the manor of Birton – Sir Barton never slept with woman or man. Next to Sir Barton, in sitting position and line of succession, was Kenneth Severs, accountant by nature and training, graduate *summa cum laude* of Harvard, American citizen, a man with a mind from which they could have launched the Early Bird satellite. On Sir Barton's right, Jacques de Blaie, younger son of the de Blaies envied by all the wine growers of the Médoc for their first-growth clarets. Jacques de Blaie had come into an inheritance of twenty million pounds sterling equivalent when he was twenty-one. Everyone thought he would buy a château and become a wine baron. Instead, he wandered the world, an international playboy, it seemed, taking up this business and that, and dropping it if it didn't seem to suit. What no one but de Blaie knew was that, as each business appeared to come and go, millions of pounds of the assets stuck to de Blaie's elegant fingers. He had an unrivalled eye for a bargain, a company in trouble, a business about to go broke. His twenty millions had become a hundred by the time he met Sir Barton. A less likely combination it would be hard to envisage. De Blaie was fun-loving, had married four times, was rarely seen without a lovely woman beside him. He wallowed in international café-society publicity, kept a yacht at Cannes in the season, had a house and a hundred-acre estate on the north side of the island of of Jamaica and a permanent suite at the Waldorf Towers and at Claridges. The only true friend he had in the world was Alec Haig.

Alec seated himself at the fourth chair at the table. He brought no papers with him, his mind a dossier of marshalled facts. It took only five minutes to present what Sir Barton called, 'The Alec Haig Report, South Wales!'

'This phosphorus-free steel, Alec,' de Blaie asked when he had finished ' – is it worth the bother, *c'est à dire, métallurgiquement*?'

66

Alec replied in French, which all understood as fluently as English, German or Spanish. 'Yes, it's worth it. With a world monopoly we could double the turnover of all our steel interests. Others will make it in time, of course, since it's a question of technique, and then the only steel people will buy will be phosphorus-free. It'll drive architects crazy when they realize they can simplify the construction of all bridges, large buildings, factories!'

'It's not just a metallurgist's pipe dream?'

'It is true to say, without exaggeration, that it will change the face of the world as we now know it.'

Sir Barton closed his file with a snap. Changing the face of the world was going a little too far for him. 'What do you propose?' he asked.

When Alec had finished his recommendations, even Sir Barton was grinning. 'Serve them right!' he said. 'Serve them jolly well right!' and then his face flushed, as if he had been caught illicitly listening to the cricket scores.

Jacques de Blaie, however, sat thoughtful. 'How like you, Alec,' he said, 'to want to dash off and tackle this thing yourself. We have good men in Japan, and you know, we wouldn't like anything to happen to you.'

'Nothing is going to happen to me,' Alec said. 'But whoever sent a man into South Wales killed one of our employees, and his wife's now got him in a ball of our steel on her mantelpiece, and that, somehow, makes this whole thing personal for me!'

They were silent, thinking of that horrible ball of steel, the last remains of Brannigan.

'Okay,' Kenneth Severs said, looking round at his fellow board members, each of whom nodded. 'As we say in my country – go get 'em.'

'I hope to do exactly that,' Alec said, his cold English voice full of a strange menace.


Françoise was waiting for him when he returned to his own office. This time the kiss took longer, and was carried out on the warm black-leather-covered sofa which took up the entire wall of her office.

'You've been away a long time,' she said, 'with those Welsh girls! I've missed you.'

'I've missed you too.'

'No, don't tell me. Show me!'

Françoise was fighting a losing battle, and somewhere in the back of her consciousness she knew it. Alec had once been in love, once had married, but that seemed a long time ago. He met Marika while he was at Göttingen – she was studying the piano with Stipulkowski, retired from the concert platform. He had conducted a wild courtship in Germany and later in America where she followed him when Stipulkowski died. They were married immediately following his course at Harvard. It was a wonderful life together for six months, until a jet plane taking her to compete in the Leeds International Piano Competition went down in the Mediterranean. Alec never got over it – when Jacques de Blaie found him he was immersed in work, day and night, driven by a compulsion of grief that would not let him rest. 'Relax,' Jacques had said, but he knew it was impossible. Men were taken many ways by tragedy. Some headed for the bottle, some for bed – others, like Alec, too disciplined for excessive drinking and too fastidious for an endless succession of pillows, drove themselves unmercifully into work – the seat at the top of the boardroom table, or an early cardiac death, their only destination. Jacques de Blaie, who always had an

68

eye for a bargain, brought him into Instecon. If this man were so determined to work, let Instecon draw the material benefit. It wasn't only that – Jacques also liked Alec from the first. The only manifestation, now, of Alec's love for Marika was, oddly enough, his insatiable appetite for beauty in all its forms, and his hatred of classical piano music.

# PHASE 15

Toni was as unlike a garage proprietor as it is possible to be. His real name was Theodore Charalambous Pappayannikas, a Cypriot Greek in love with all things mechanical. He kept a garage on the crest of the mountain overlooking Zürich. He was out at seven o'clock when Alec and Françoise arrived, but two minutes later, came roaring back in an ancient *deux* '*cheveux*' that somehow he managed to make sound like a supercharged Aston Martin.

'Three kilometres,' he said, bursting with good-humoured rage, 'and the bastard had forgotten to buy petrol!' He grasped Alec's hand. '*Ciao!*' he said, and turned to Françoise and whistled. Together he and Alec went into the littered workshop behind the garage itself. 'What do you want this time?' he asked.

'A gun!'

'But guns, as you know, are not my business.'

'A special gun. Do you know these nailing guns that fire a steel nail into a girder, or into concrete?'

'One little cartridge, a tap or pull the trigger, and pow! the nail is in.'

'That's right – but you can forget the cartridge.'

'Makes a noise, eh?'

'That's right. What do you think?'

'Compressed air. Pump it up, press the trigger, and pow!'

'How silent?'

'Perfectly silent – until the nail goes in, and that's something neither you nor I can do anything about.'

'What would it sound like?'

Toni took a hammer, a thin-bladed riveting hammer, and tapped the surface of an anvil on the floor. The metallic clang was noticeable, but not loud.

'That will do fine,' Alec said.

'I suppose as usual you want this thing small enough to go in your pocket?'

'Of course!'

'And, as usual, you want it today.'

'Of course.'

Toni went to the door of the workshop. 'Pretty lady,' he called. Françoise came in. 'Pretty lady,' he repeated, 'go into that cesspool I call a kitchen and bring out a bottle of *ouzo* you'll find on the table, and three glasses. This is going to take a little time.'

'You'll need to wash the glasses,' Alec told her with a laugh.

Toni punched his arm. 'Now – what are you going to fire, and into what are you going to fire it?'

Françoise spent twenty minutes in the kitchen, washing the used plates and cutlery Toni had obviously been piling up for at least a week. When she came back into the workshop they had just finished. So engrossed had they been that neither appeared to have missed her, or the *ouzo*.

Françoise and Alec ate dinner at one of the restaurants on the south side of the Zürich lake, at a table by the window. Françoise, sensing a need in Alec, talked throughout the entire meal in her witty way. Alec responded to her but, unusually, made no attempt to entertain her. When the meal was over, she lit a cigarette for him and passed it over the table. He caught her eyes, and smiled ruefully. 'I've not been very good company, have I?' he asked. She reached across the table cloth and put her hand on his. 'Don't worry. I know you are upset about something, and if you want to, you'll tell me.' He looked across the table at her, this lovely girl who had so frequently given herself to him, who shared everything she could with him, who held nothing back, and demanded so little.

'I'm worried about South Wales,' he said ' – I don't like that murder. It seems so brutally unnecessary. All right, there was an intruder, and he was surprised by one of our workmen, but he could have knocked him out – he didn't need to kill him!'

'Unless . . .'

'Unless what?' His manner was short, angry.

'Unless the intruder recognized him.'

'But why? If the intruder recognized him, that means he was someone who worked on the Bessemer plant, and he could have photographed the papers at any time.' But then, the light dawned. 'Of course, there's no way of knowing it was someone from the Bessemer. South Wales is such a close-knit community, he could have been from another part of the works, and therefore had no right to be on the Bessemer platform anyway.'

He was deep in thought. Françoise had taken her hand from his, and was searching in her handbag. Not lifting her head, so that he couldn't see her face, she said – 'That's not what is really bothering you, though, is it?'

'What do you mean?'

She had found what she was looking for, took it out of her handbag, and placed it on the table by his hand. It was a key, a flat key for a Yale lock.

'I had that key cut specially for you,' she said, 'to take away with you. Possibly while you're away it will remind you of me.

72

When you come back – you might, you just might, like to use it. Next time you go away, while you're abroad I'm going to ask them to transfer me out of the Technical Sales section, so we shan't be talking together on business matters.' There was a catch in her voice. 'It's the key to my flat.' He started to speak, but she stopped him. 'I may be making the biggest mistake of my life,' she said, 'because I believe this is what is called "making demands on you"! I don't want us to be able to talk about business any more, only to talk about ourselves. And I suppose that means that, in my own stupid silly way, I'm proposing to you!' Still she wouldn't let him speak. 'If this thing you're doing is going to involve murder – one day the man they murder might be you, and if that is going to happen, I want to have been married to you!'

There were bright tears in her eyes. He reached across the table and put his hand on her cheek.

'How do you want it, Françoise?'

'Straight!'

'I think you should wait, and give this key to someone else.'

---

Sally had just returned from seeing Samuel Reynolds when the telex in the corner of her office, outside what had been his office, began to clatter. His office was now occupied by Mr Sodaberg, who had brought over his own secretary from Zürich. She worked inside the office with him, lived in a hotel in town, and never mixed with other company personnel. Sally let the telex finish its message, tore off the sheet, and was about to take it in to Mr Sodaberg, the only man who received these top priority messages always in code, when she saw it was in clear language, and addressed to her. The message it carried was, at first, unbelievable.

ASSUMING PASSPORT OKAY WILL MEET YOU OFF SAS 66 LONDON COPENHAGEN NINE AYEM TUESDAY STOP PACK FOR SEVEN DAYS INCLUDING SOCIAL WEAR SIGNED ALEC HAIG

She had just finished reading when the telex started to chatter again. This time the message was addressed to the cashier, and still uncoded.

AUTHORIZE EXPENSES ADVANCE ONE HUNDRED (£100) CODE AH/TS (MISC) MISS SALLY MICHAELS SIGNED ALEC HAIG

As casual as that! Pick up a hundred pounds and your passport, and come to Copenhagen. Sally still believed it some kind of off-beat joke when she showed the authorization to the cashier. It became reality as he counted ten ten-pound notes into her hand, and got her to sign a form headed 'Advance on Expenses'.

'Save as many vouchers as you can, Miss,' he said. 'It makes it so much easier.'

So that was how these high-flying international types did it, she thought! A week-end at Brighton, jet-set style. But what a shock Mr High-Fly Haig had coming to him – in Copenhagen!

He was waiting at the foot of the gangplank as the plane taxied in. She walked down the ramp feeling none of the determined self-composure with which she had started out the previous evening. A night in the glamorous airport hotel had done nothing to allay her suspicions and fears. The restaurant had been crowded with expense-account travellers, wining and dining glossy, if somewhat shop-soiled, companions. 'Is this what I'm likely to turn into?' she asked herself, knowing that honour is very often no more than a measure of lack of temptation. Somehow, she was angry with him for being at the bottom of the gangway. 'At least, he might have let me powder my nose,' she thought. But as he whisked her briskly through the immigration hall and the Customs – so different from when she had arrived in Barcelona on her two weeks on the Costa Brava annual holiday last year – she quickly composed herself, and no one could have known the turmoil going on inside her.

Once through the Customs, he turned his attentions to her. 'We're leaving again in two hours,' he said, 'but it was worth clearing your luggage.'

'Leaving? Where are we going?'

'Tokyo!'

'Tokyo?'

'Yes, Tokyo. And it'll make it easier for you if you try not to repeat everything I say!' It was not a snub, delivered as it was with such a warm cheering smile. Sally was out of her depth, but her small-town Welsh sensibility took over. She allowed herself to be taken in to breakfast, and made no protest when he loaded her plate with a Scandinavian smörgåsbord breakfast that normally would have sunk her without trace. Afterwards, he took her solicitously on a tour of the airport shops.

'What will the weather be like, in Tokyo?' she asked.

When he said warm and sunny, she bought a light cardigan, and a thin sleeveless blouse. For the first time she used Company money. All her expenses so far she had paid from her own pocket, bolstered by the thought of his expression when she threw the telex message and the ten tenners into his face. That would be right after she had slapped it, the first time he made a pass at her!

Once seated on the over-the-Pole Copenhagen-to-Tokyo direct flight and able to relax, the doubt came pressing in. He showed no sign of explaining anything to her. He had kept a slim suitcase on the plane with him, and was reading the documents it contained. From time to time she glanced at him. Distinguished, that's what he looked. It had taken her a long time to find the right word, the right description, but that was it. He was handsome, certainly, but had none of that gloss that shows up inevitably as lack of character. Nor was he particularly attractive – you could see him in a crowd and not be particularly aware of him. But, sitting alone like this, nestling in the curve of their first-class seats, he looked distinguished.

'Made up your mind?' he asked quietly.

She was quickly embarrassed. 'Sorry, was I staring?'

'No,' he said. 'You've been brought up much too well to stare. You've been peeping!'

'I'm sorry,' she said, her smile belying her contrition.

'No, you're not,' he said. 'And anyway, you have every right to peep. Not every girl would have accepted being

76

pulled from her home at a moment's notice, and taken half way round the world by a strange man.'

'You think I ought to have protested?'

'Outraged virtue? Not your style at all!' Guiltily she felt the ten-pound notes in her pocket, the telex message she had meant to fling in his face. 'Mind you, I imagine you could be a tough tiger if it became necessary.' He smiled at her and put his hand on hers.

'Will it become necessary?' she asked softly.

'I don't know.'

'At least you're honest!'

He looked around the plane. In their double seat they might have been alone in a sound-proofed room. Some things he would need to tell her; other things she'd better not know.

His hand stayed on hers for another minute while neither spoke. Then he opened the suitcase again. 'Right, back to business. I am Head of the Technical Sales Department of Instecon. You were the secretary of the former Managing Director of Instecon South Wales. I am going to Japan to look at a steel works there. You are coming as my secretary. You have said you would like to work for the Technical Sales Department. We are giving you a chance to show if you are any good at the job. Is that clear?' His voice was all business, bereft of any of those personal resonances which had so intrigued her.

'Fact, or fiction?' she asked.

'Fact! I have in my bag an application you have made to me to be considered for the Technical Sales section. This application came through the Personnel Department, of course, and was forwarded through the usual channels.'

'Let me see that,' she said.

He held out the typewritten piece of paper. It was signed with a rough facsimile of her own signature. 'I never signed that,' she denied, hotly. He put his hand on her arm again. 'I know you didn't,' he said, 'and you know you didn't, but no one else does!'

She turned in her seat and looked him full in the face. When she spoke, she kept her voice down, but there was no denying the intensity of it. 'You're not a technical salesman,' she said, 'and I'm not a secretary! Not any more. For a start, I was permitted to leave the country with £100! Instecon fixed that, I suppose. There's something going on, and I demand to be told.'

'Or?'

'Or, I . . .' Emotions struggled within her. Desperately she wanted to trust him, to have complete faith in him, but it was so soon. They were alone here; he could be frank!

'Or?'

'I would like to know as much as you feel you can trust me to know.'

'That's better,' he said, and opened a file in his suitcase.

'You're a hard man!' He looked about them.

'Believe me, I need to be. Now listen! As you know, South Wales has developed a new kind of steel, phosphorus free.' It pleased her to hear him speak of the factory in which she had always worked as South Wales. Somehow it put her on his side of the fence. 'The secret of that steel has been stolen by the Japanese, and it is now being manufactured in the Mitziguchi steel works, where we are going. I want to find out how they got the secret of Wales Steel, and in case I run into any sex barriers, I want you there to help me!'

'Sex barriers! You mean I'm to be some sort of geisha girl?'

'No,' he said. 'If we need it, you're the one who looks in the ladies' toilet! Provided they have such a thing.'

Both laughed, the tension broken.

78

'Principally,' he said, 'I want you there for three reasons. One is the "sex barrier" – two is in case you recognize anyone who at any time has visited Mr Reynolds in Wales, and three, well, we'll stay off three, shall we?'

'For the moment?' she asked, *sotto voce*.

'For as long as possible!' he said, thinking of Françoise.

It would be a long time before he could forgive himself for the incident of the key – but he knew he had been right. Brutal, possibly, but right! Françoise had given him too much honesty to be deceived at that moment. She had been right, of course, when she said offering the key could be a mistake, but what kind of man could live his life, especially now that murder had stalked into it, knowing that on the other side of a front door a woman was waiting for the sound of his key or the ring of a telegram messenger.

He knew that, in the future, either was possible.

Or neither.

# PHASE 17

Within fifteen minutes of their arrival in Tokyo they had been photographed by one of Kotaro's men. They checked into the Tokyo International Hotel, an oriental replica of the International Hotels everywhere. Sally was pleased with it. To have conformed to Japanese standards in the sanctity of her hotel room would have been too much for her. She was comforted, rather than intimidated, when Alec booked them into a suite with two bedrooms opening off one sitting-room. At least, each had a private bathroom! And there was a lock on her bedroom door.

The first evening they dined, alone, in the public restaurant, and after coffee she went early to bed. It had been a tiring flight, too exciting for her to get much sleep. Tokyo had been a blaze of coloured lights when they came in to land – seen from the air it looked like any other airport, though she could not know that. Her first taste of Japanese came at Haneda Airport, and since that moment her head had whirled with the exotic sights and sounds of the city. She fell asleep almost as soon as her head touched the pillow. For some reason she had not locked her door.

Alec was in the communal sitting-room when a tap came on the door. He opened it to admit two men, Katsuhiro Kai, and Antonio Giovanni, recently arrived from South America via Seattle, Washington State.

'Keep it quiet,' Alec said, indicating the closed bedroom

door. Katsuhiro grinned. 'Local Japanese girl?' he asked. Alec smiled back at him. 'No, imported!' Katsuhiro made a grimace of disappointment. Antonio Giovanni had been prowling around the room, looking under the telephones and the lampshades, and behind the Japanese prints on the wall. He even unscrewed the light bulb from its socket. Alec watched him in quiet amusement, then, 'Here, catch this!' he said, and threw Toni's gun across the room to him. Giovanni, the old hand, didn't catch the gun but batted it with his open palm so it fell harmlessly on to the sofa. Then he bent down and examined it carefully before picking it up.

'Another toy for me?' he asked.

'That's right. You'll hear all about it later.'

Alec took a small box from his pocket and handed it to Antonio. It contained pyramid-shaped pieces of what looked and felt like metal tacks, with a base about a tenth of an inch across and a height of a quarter of an inch. There were hundreds of them in the box.

'Whom should I meet at Mitziguchi?' he asked Katsuhiro.

'You'll have to talk to everybody. They'll put on a special display for you. I told them you were thinking of buying ingots to ship to Australia for cold rolling, provided they could come up with an interesting steel. They said why couldn't you ship ingots from Europe, particularly South Wales, but I said your ingot capacity was fully taken up. I don't think they believed me. You'll have to watch yourself.'

'I always do.'

'In particular, watch out for a man called Kotaro Hitohori.' Katsuhiro produced a photograph, obviously taken from a distance with a telephoto lens. 'He was once a communications expert, but now he seems to be high up in the Mitziguchi management.'

'What specially do you want me to do?' Giovanni asked,

satisfied now he had made certain the room had not been bugged.

'I want you to go into and out of the Mitziguchi steel works, by as many different routes as you can find. And I don't want anyone to know you have been in there.'

'Don't worry, they won't. What am I looking for?'

'I don't know, yet. I may know when I've been in there, officially. I may want to go back in there, unofficially, but by a safe route!'

'Leave it to me,' Antonio said. 'Give me one night, and I'll know the ways in and out better than you know the maze at Hampton Court!'

'I hope so,' Alec said, smiling. 'I've never been in the maze at Hampton Court!'

When the two men had gone, Alec poured himself a glass of whisky, diluted with cold tap water despite the ice in the thermos container. He sat down by the window, and let the sight and sounds of the cool Tokyo night relax him. Not far from his hotel was the Ginza – the saddest mile of pulchritude in the entire world. He looked momentarily and speculatively at the closed door of Sally's bedroom, but then drained his drink and went to his own bed on the other side of the suite.

# PHASE 18

The following morning a Mitziguchi Company car was waiting outside the International Hotel to take Alec and his secretary to the steel works, about fifteen miles outside Tokyo on the coast road towards Funabashi and Chiba. On the way they passed the head offices of Fuji Iron and Steel Company, and Yawata, both among the largest steel companies in Japan. 'We have a fine relationship with those two companies,' Alec said, 'though we're fighting them like hell for the Common Market countries business!' Acting out his role as a technical salesman, Alec would have to pay courtesy calls on them while he was in Tokyo. The driver of the Datsun appeared to speak no English, but a sudden pressure on Sally's knee, and the shake of Alec's head, had warned her to limit their conversation to topical generalities. For Sally, this entire trip had taken on the aspect of a fantasy, a magical dream in which she appeared to float on a cloud of luxury. The first surprise had come when she had changed money in the hotel, and had been given notes with a face value of ten thousand yen. The value didn't decrease when she realized they were worth only the equivalent of ten pounds. From the side window of her bedroom, on a corner of the hotel, she could see on one side the Ginza, the main street of Tokyo, and on the other side the slopes of Mount Fuji. The maid who came to turn down her bed, dressed excitingly in a Japanese robe, had beckoned through the window. 'Fuji-san,' she said,

'Fuji-san!' and then she giggled and bowed her way out of the room.

'When we get back to the hotel tonight,' she said, 'if you don't want me for any work, I really must take a walk. Do you realize, I've done no walking at all since I left South Wales!'

'It's a foolish life, that of the rich,' Alec said. 'We never walk anywhere, and so we take up squash and fencing, and we pull away at artificial rowing machines to try to keep our bodies in trim. We eat monstrous amounts of the most unsuitable foods, and then we diet and take pills to get rid of the ill effects. And yet here you are, three miles of walking a day, and no doubt simple but wholesome food at home, and you're as trim as a gazelle, with a complexion any woman would envy.' He reached out his hand and stroked her cheek. '*Ni nardas ni caracolas, tienen el cutis tan fino,*' he said. And to his utter surprise she added, 'Are you going to take me by the river and give me a basket of silks . . . ?' She laughed at his discomfiture – the expression of surprise on his face. 'We have books in South Wales, you know, and they're not all written by Gwyn Thomas!'

Kotaro Hitohori himself was waiting for them when they arrived in the steel works. They had expected a round of Japanese courtesy – sitting on cushions and watching Geisha girls was the way Sally had imagined it – but Kotaro was all business, all western world. He was wearing, as were most of the men they had seen on the streets, a normal business suit. As he showed them round the offices Sally was surprised to note that all the girls, too, were wearing dresses and two-piece costumes, shirts, blouses, jumpers, in the styles she was accustomed to. Somehow, it seemed disappointing. 'I should have worn a mini-skirt! That would have shaken them,' she thought. Their tour of the works lasted all morning. Alec

84

asked many questions on his way round and it soon became apparent Kotaro knew as much about steel making as he did. Alec restrained an impulse to frown when Kotaro boasted to him about their new steel – which contained, or so he said, absolutely no 'flosflolus'. 'And we thought we were the only people who had that secret,' Alec urbanely remarked. Kotaro smiled and bowed his head. It seemed he was anxious to show them everything in the Mitziguchi steel works. 'You will meet the management later this afternoon,' he explained, 'after Haig-san has seen everything he wants to see.' Alec groaned. That would mean hours of sitting on cushions in the Japanese tea-garden he had seen behind the office block, with hardly a word being spoken. One thing, however, he didn't ask to see, and Kotaro didn't volunteer to show him. A large aluminium balloon was mounted at the top of a very high tower. On it was written the word Mitziguchi in Japanese and in English. It looked no more than an elegant advertisement. Beneath it was the conventional water tank, in concrete, to contain the large volumes of water needed quickly to quench coke from the ovens. But projecting from the aluminium sphere were many small stub rods, and he could guess that in the tower were amplifiers for the world-spanning antennae of which those rods were a vital part. Somewhere in the works was a communications room, of very advanced design, to judge from the complex Hamay antonnae set-up, those ears on space that could track even a satellite.

Kotaro himself rode back into Tokyo with them when finally, in the early evening, they were able to leave the Japanese tea-party given in their honour. He had other business to do in the centre of the city, he explained. When they arrived at the hotel Sally went immediately up to their suite. 'I imagine you'd like a good European gin and tonic!' Kotaro suggested, and they went into the bar.

'A very attractive girl,' Kotaro said, when they were sipping their drinks. 'I understand she works in your Welsh subsidiary?'

He's done his homework quickly, Alec thought.

'Whereas you work in the Zürich Head Office, in the Technical Sales Department?'

'That's right,' Alec said. 'It says so on my card!'

Kotaro thought for a while. 'There are doubtless many things it does not say on your card, Mr Haig?' There was no doubting the change in his silky voice. 'Here it comes,' Alec thought. 'What is it to be, a threat or a proposition?'

'But then, there are many things best left unsaid, are there not? You yourself are skilled in the way of not saying, are you not, Haig-san. You must have seen a lot today that made you wish to comment – the efficiency of our blast furnace techniques, our strip rolling mill, our . . .' and here he paused almost imperceptibly, 'flosflolus-flee steel!'

'There's an old European saying, Hitohori-san, that it's no use crying over spilt milk!'

Kotaro's face split in a smile, and he nodded wisely. 'I hope you will both have a very pleasant stay in Japan, and I am at your disposal at any time. I think you will both arrive home safely,' he said, finished his drink, and left abruptly.

Sally was in the shower when Alec arrived in their suite. She came out wrapped in a pale lemon towelling dressing gown, her auburn hair piled on the top of her head, loosely held by the knotted wisp of a chiffon scarf.

'Do you realize this is the first time we've been alone together all day?' she asked impatiently. He looked surprised, then she understood what she had implied and laughed unaffectedly. 'That sounds a terrible thing to say, I mean, as if I was waiting to be, well . . .'

He walked over to her. 'Don't bother,' he said, and kissed

86

her gently on the tip of her nose. 'I know what you mean. Now tell me, did you see anyone there you have also seen in South Wales?'

'I've been dying to tell you all day!'

'Who was it?'

'Mr Hittyhorry, or whatever his name is!'

'Hitohori? Are you sure?'

'Positive!'

Alec went into his bedroom, and he too took a shower. It had been hot out at the steel works, and dusty, and sitting in the heated garden had been a refined torture. When he came out of his bedroom, dressed for a comfortable evening in a pair of slacks and a cashmere jersey shirt, Sally had disappeared. He searched her bedroom, her bathroom, but there was no trace of her. He went out into the corridor and downstairs in the lift. She was not in the main entrance hall, not in the dining-room, and then, suddenly, he saw her sitting in a dark corner of the bar. With Hitohori! They were talking together, earnestly. Alec ducked out of sight and went back across the lounge. There was a row of telephone booths along one corner wall. He went in one, sat down on the leather-covered stool, leaving the door slightly open to prevent the automatic light coming on again, and picked up the telephone. He waited, cramped in there, for half an hour, and then on a sudden suspicion came out of the booth and crossed the lounge to where he could see into the bar. The chairs they had occupied were empty. He walked rapidly across to the bar. Behind the bar, out of sight of the main door, a second entrance led down a small flight of steps into the street.

# PHASE 19

It is amazing what you can discover if you sit in the pubs, drinking slowly, watching, listening, talking a little, playing a game of darts, and moving, slowly moving over the ebb and flow of humanity, sifting a word there, a word here, some things not said, people arriving and leaving quickly, people arriving and not talking, people leaving talking quietly, a word, no more, a nod of compliance, then drink up and go. Frank was fascinated by it. Within two hours of opening time, he knew that the Free Society had a special meeting on that night. He knew also it was not an official meeting, since the local organizer was to be told nothing of it. Even Elwyn himself appeared to know nothing of it. Shortly after Frank arrived at the Heads of the Valley, a popular pub out on the Brynfyn road, he noticed a small party of men assembling in the public bar, all drinking pints of beer. He would have thought nothing of it but one of the men looked constantly at the clock above the bar. Finally a fifth man arrived – Frank knew him slightly, he worked on the blast furnace – and made a quiet apology. Frank heard him refer to 'the missis' and the man who'd been looking at the clock laughed. It was a grim laugh. When the five men left, a couple of minutes later, Frank finished his drink, and left shortly behind them. They were walking up the Brynfyn road, past the row of workmen's cottages on the edge of the road itself, with the side of the valley dropping sheer away behind them. Obviously unused to secrecy the men made no attempt to hide themselves, and Frank had no difficulty keeping a hundred yards behind them. Past the end of the row of cottages they turned right, along the hog's back of the edge of the valley itself. 'That road goes to only one place,' Frank thought. 'The Cefn Arms.' The Cefn Arms was a small pub-*cum*-club that stood on its own at the end of the track above the valley's edge, much favoured by steel workers since it opened, unofficially of course, on a Sunday. It was so isolated that police could never approach it without being seen. It was even rumoured that a bit of gambling went on there from time to time and, in the old days of course, cock-fighting. Frank decided to trust his instinct and carried straight on up the road. When he was out of sight of the turning he started to run, over the crest of the hill, down by the Brynfyn cinema (though why Brynfyn should qualify for a cinema no one would ever know) and over the top of the moor-like fields to drop down on the Cefn Arms from the back, the way the illicit drinkers had always left in rare times of emergency. By running, he was within sight of the Cefn Arms before the five men arrived. He let them get in, and then crossed the field behind the pub. Two dogs in the kennels at the back of the pub started barking – but it was a useless cry – the dogs would bark at anything and the landlord had long resigned himself to the fact and never came out to investigate. Soon Frank was able to stand up against the back wall of the pub, by the curtained window of the Long Room. Through the curtains he could see that some sort of meeting had started on the arrival of the five men. From the hot angry voices almost immediately raised in argument, he realized why neither the organizer of the Free Society nor Elwyn himself had been invited – this was a breakaway rebellious group, militant to judge by the anger, with sabotage the word used more often than any other.

This was Wales for the Welsh with a vengeance, brutal, ugly.

It was eleven o'clock when the meeting broke up. Frank had heard nothing definite about any specific acts of sabotage, other than congratulations to someone called Joe about the coke oven, but the mood of the meeting had been fierce, destructive and impatient. When the meeting started to break up he skipped round the side of the pub and found a garage at the front from inside which he could watch the men leave. He took an envelope and a scrap of paper from his pocket. As the men left, he noted the names. They were all familiar faces – one was blast furnace, another strip mill, another cold rolling. When they had all left, he too left, via the back route.

Back in the lighted street he ran his eye down the list of names and descriptions. There was only one Joe – Joe Michaels, from steel sheet packing plant.

Pamela was amazed to see him. 'At this time of night! How have you managed?'

'I've got a spare time job, driving a taxi!' That was how he had explained the increased income to his wife, and the fact that he could use Alec Haig's rented car whenever he needed.

Pamela hugged him close and nibbled his ear. 'So, all I have to do is to call for a taxi, eh? That's what I call doing it in style!'

'Who knows?' he said. 'I might even have to make some all-night runs up to London!'

'Poor old lad!' she said, chuckling. 'You'll be working yourself to death!'

Later, lying side by side together in bed, his face close to her face, he looked into her eyes. 'Pamela,' he said, 'do you trust me?'

She looked surprised at him and then, noting the seriousness of his expression, she thought for a moment. 'Yes,' she said. 'I think I do. I trust you certainly more than any other man I've ever known. Why?'

'What do you think about the Free Society?' he asked.

'I don't like it,' she said. 'In the first place, Wales could do with a bit of waking up, and in the second place there's some odd things going on in the name of the Free Society. Things the organizers know nothing about.'

He told her what he had discovered at the Cefn Arms.

'I think the Joe they were talking about is Joe Michaels.'

'I wouldn't be surprised,' she said. 'He's always been a fanatic, that one. And he's got a bit of a wandering eye. He had Megan Beynon for years as his tally – do anything for him, would Megan, and she no older than that daughter of his, and still it wasn't enough and he was messing about up in Brynfyn. One of the lads from the rolling mills came off work during the night with a cut hand, and went home and caught Joe Michaels, and they say he broke his cut hand on Joe Michaels' jaw. Of course, it was all hushed up.'

'How would you like to be Joe Michaels' next tally?' he said, his voice grave.

Pamela laughed at him. 'Not for me, thank you,' she said. 'That rooster's been in too many nests as it is – I'm not having him in this one.'

He looked long and hard at her, made his decision, and told her about his conversation with Alec Haig, and his mission in tracking the breakaway group.

'Fancy you! Dai the spy!' she said, half seriously.

'I'm not a spy, I'm a source of local information!'

'And Joe Michaels – killing his own workmates like that. Fanatic, that's what he is! I'd be glad to help you do him down.'

'It'll be dangerous, mind! He's killed once – he'd kill again!'

'Then you'll have to keep an eye open for me, won't you?' she said.

# PHASE 20

Antonio Giovanni had made a plan of the Mitziguchi Steel Works on the table in Alec's bedroom. 'There are only two ways in,' he said, 'but they are very simple. It would appear that internal security is something they've never even thought about.'

'Too busy listening on their radio, I expect,' Alec said grimly. Antonio had done his job well and had plotted an exact route into and out of the steel works. No doubt secure in being an island, the Japanese had relied on high walls to keep out unwanted strangers. There appeared to be no guards patrolling the walls at all, and, so far as Antonio could discover, no electronic watchdogs – no secret rays to sound warning alarms. Nor was there any sign of closed circuit television cameras watching for intruders.

'Your main problem,' he said, 'will be your height, and the colour of your skin, so you won't be able to stroll about there innocently as you could in the bustle of a European steel works.'

'What did you make of the radio tower?'

'As you thought,' Giovanni reported. 'Aerials, also satellite tracking antennae. You'd never guess where the control room is.'

'In the concrete water tank below!'

Giovanni looked disappointed. Alec smiled at him. 'That

water tank is out of all proportion to the size of the coking ovens!' he said. 'There had to be something else in it, and I was certain it couldn't be a swimming pool! Have you got the pictures yet?'

'No, Katsuhiro Kai is bringing them – he should be here at any moment.'

Through the partly open door into the suite Alec heard a sudden movement, and then the door opened and Sally appeared. 'If you don't want me for anything,' she said, 'I think I'll take a walk.'

'You'll have no soles left on your shoes,' he said. 'We'll have dinner late, if you'd prefer.' She nodded and went out.

He walked over to the window, which overlooked the front of the hotel. In a few minutes he saw her stroll along under the canopy and turn left into the street. After a few seconds a figure detached itself from the wall beside the doorway and walked along the street in the direction she was taking. Alec looked to the other side of the street. A Japanese waiting in the shadow of the garish neon of the Chome Emporium glanced quickly up at the suite where Alec was standing at the window, and then he too walked in the direction taken by the girl and the man following her.

'Now why is Kotaro having her followed and not me?' Alec asked.

'Because you don't spend two hours every evening, just walking!'

'I wasn't brought up as a Welsh mountain goat!'

'I don't understand the simile – there's nothing mountain-goat-like about Miss Michaels.'

'No, there isn't, is there,' Alec mused.

There was a tap on the door into the corridor. Katsuhiro

Kai came in. From his pocket he produced enlargements of the photographs Giovanni had taken inside the Mitziguchi steel works. There was a smile on his face. 'Everything must go very easily,' he said. He held up one of the photographs of the radio-*cum*-water-tower. 'See that man coming out of the door at the foot of the tower?' he asked. Both could see the figure quite clearly. To them, he looked like any other Japanese. 'Radio operator during the war,' Kai said, the huge grin still on his face. 'A man of no honour, also much married to my cousin!'

Giovanni bent over his black leather bag of tricks. From it he produced a brass cap. He took an electric light bulb from the bed and screwed it into the cap. Then he screwed the cap and the bulb back into the bed-head socket. The light came on again. From his leather case he brought a small transistor radio. He opened the top. In it was a miniature tape recorder. He turned on the radio and from it came the music of one of the Tokyo radio stations, a Japanese pop group singing a Beatles song in Japanese. When he pressed a part of the transistor's case the music stopped and there was silence. Alec and Katsuhiro looked mystified, and then Giovanni placed his head about four feet from the bed-head light bulb and started softly to sing, '*Tre giorni mia ninetta acciò non dorma più* . . .' and the sound of his Neapolitan voice came to them from the transistor radio. As soon as his voice started, the tape recorder jerked into activity. When he stopped singing, the tape recorder stopped. He wound it back and played it again. His voice had been recorded faithfully, missing only the first part of the first word.

'There's a microphone in the socket connector, and a miniaturized transmitter. It works off the mains.'

'What range?' Alec asked.

'Three miles.'

'There's a lot of metal about in the steel works,' Alec warned him.

'There's a lot of power in this little gadget,' he said, unperturbed. 'Don't forget it's mains operated.'

Alec turned to Kai. 'Have you anywhere you can plant the receiver – within two miles of the Mitziguchi main gate?'

Kai nodded. Alec took the brass socket connector and gave it to him. 'Let's hope your cousin's husband knows how to change an electric light bulb!' he said.

Alec was standing by the window, looking down at the street. 'That's strange,' he said. 'Kotaro's man – he's back. And there's no sign of your man, or Sally!'

Giovanni crossed to the window and looked down. He spotted the man almost instantly – 'See the way he's looking up and down the street, uncertain? He's lost her!'

'They won't like that at Mitziguchi,' Katsuhiro said, as they left the room to look for the man, much married to his cousin, they had identified from the photograph.

They took a taxi – one of the small Citroëns named Kamikazi taxis from the way the drivers push them like madmen along the narrow streets – into the streets that branch off from the Ginza. The taxi stopped outside a small theatre decorated with garish neon lights and a showcase of photographs of actors of the old-style Japanese theatre, a few actresses in kimonos and girls wearing G-strings and not much else. Inside, the stage was set across one wall of the room, and seats were spread, starting at some distance from the stage itself. There was none of the café atmosphere of such places in the West – from the arrangement of the seats, and the strip of stage that extended like a tongue out towards the audience, it was apparent the spectators were here for one purpose alone, to watch the girls. There were a few sideways glances when Alec Haig walked into the room and stood with Katsuhiro against one wall – he was the only foreigner. The performance started with a traditional playlet, the girls all heavily kimonoed. Though Alec couldn't understand a word of Japanese, the plot was sufficiently bawdy for him to follow it by gesture alone. The two men on the stage were opposite in sexual ability, or so the plot suggested, and one man was determined that the other man should be aroused by their several companions. The girls, however, were anxious to profit by the first man's ability and endowments, without wasting effort and interest on the second. One of the girls, however, rejected by the virile man, appeared to take pity on his less fortunate friend, and by skilful temptation brought him to a state of pride. When the other girls realized this, they abandoned the virile man for his companion. It was an excessively simple plot, yet Alec was interested by the great efforts of mime the girls put into their performance. No part of the show would have passed a censor in the 'civilized' western world, but Alec found its flagrant bawdiness amusing. One of the girls then came along the 'catwalk' leading from the stage towards the audience, and began to unfold the *obi* from her kimono. It was apparent the girl would not have much to reveal, and the audience lacked interest in her. Just before the final black-out, she let the kimono fall from her shoulder and momentarily revealed one tiny breast. The revelation was greeted without applause by the audience. 'They're waiting for the western style!' Katsuhiro whispered to Alec. 'This is traditional Japanese style, and no one is really interested.'

Excitement soon began to mount when the lights were switched on again, and the curtains parted to reveal a European girl, dressed in a long silk dress whose skirt was slit to the waist. What she lacked in style, Alec thought, she made up for in energy as she bumped and ground her way through the routines of an early Chicago stripper. The men of the audience, few of whom in the front rows could have been older than thirty, were delighted with her, especially when she came out on the catwalk and squatted down before them, revealing even her most intimate parts at close quarters.

Alec felt himself grow hot under the collar. By no means a prude, he was nauseated by the prurient performance and the obvious carnal delight of the audience.

'Is your cousin's husband here?' he asked Katsuhiro.

Katsuhiro smiled in enjoyment, and gestured to the man before whom the stripper was making her lewd obeisance. Then he reached into his pocket and drew out what looked like a large cigarette lighter. Under cover of the semi-darkness and confident everyone's attention would be directed at only one tiny place in the room, he brought the device momentarily to his eye. It was a black light camera, and on the tiny frame of film his cousin's face would be captured fore-shortened into close proximity with the body of the stripper, in her revealing pose. 'That's just in case he objects to working for us,' he said to Alec as they left to wait in the less fetid atmosphere of the street outside. When they were standing in a darkened doorway, from which they could see the front of the theatre, Alec held out his hand. 'Give me that piece of film,' he instructed. Katsuhiro wound it through the camera and handed over the tiny capsule.

'If he won't work for us for money,' Alec said, 'I'd rather not use that particular piece of film.'

Katsuhiro looked at him – the ways of foreigners was, as ever, unpredictable. Alec saw the look, and smiled ruefully.

'I know what you're thinking,' he said; 'but there are

levels I won't go down to, and that's one of them. Don't ask me how I can justify it, because I can't, but any man we have to blackmail into working for us, I don't want!'

# PHASE 21

Sally was wearing slacks when they left for the Mitziguchi Steel Works the following morning. 'Today is going to be tough,' Alec said. 'Today we're really going to get our hands dirty!'

Kotaro was waiting for them again at the main gate. Alec caught a look flash between him and Sally. 'Invite her out for dinner, would you, you bastard?' he thought. He was quite surprised to discover in himself a sudden explosion of jealousy. They transferred from the Datsun that had brought them from Tokyo, into an American Willys, a later and better upholstered model of the jeep.

'Where would Haig-san care to go first?' Kotaro asked, beaming.

'Let's start at the back end first,' Alec said, 'and see the rolling mills.' Mitziguchi was one of the few Japanese steel plants which are integrated, that is, at which they not only make the steel from iron ore, but also roll the steel into sheets, pipework, coils, etc. 'Better still,' Kotaro said, 'since you don't have such a plant at South Wales, let us look at the flanged tubing mill.'

Kotaro gave instructions to the Japanese driver, sitting inscrutably behind the wheel, and they drove off down the waterfront road, past the ore wharves and the lime wharf, to a long low building about a mile from the main gate. Inside, the building was dark, and about fifty men scurried backwards and forwards, a great contrast to the normal activity inside a steel works, where a few men often cope with the output of a plant capable of delivering hundreds of tons of molten metal an hour. Here the plant stretched out in one long row. At the near end of the row were coils, five feet in diameter, of steel about five inches wide. Above the coils an overhead gantry could lift a single coil and carry it to the end of the line. The steel on the giant bobbins slowly unwound and passed first into a long low gas-heated furnace about forty feet long. The steel ribbon moved faster than walking pace, and mustn't be allowed to slow down once it got inside the furnace. Several men danced about the bobbins, ensuring that the unwinding was steady, standing back quickly to weld another coil on to the end of the one passing through the furnace, to maintain a continuous feed. At the far end of the furnace the coil emerged white hot and passed immediately through the wheel-shaped blades of a bending machine, which twisted the ribbon into a continuous U. The next bending machine put two flanges on the ends of the U, and a third machine bent the U into an O shape. The last machine rubbed the two flanges together, so that the ribbon emitting from the end of the last bending machine was formed into a perfect pipe with a flange running along its length. Standing by the machine were twenty men. Another ten men were tending the machines. The ribbon ran through them, gleaming white hot, and perspiration poured from the men's bodies as the ribbon snaked not a foot from them. Each man tending the machines held a large hammer. By the first machine, immediately after the end of the oven, stood a man with a large axe, behind him in neat files a group of men holding tongs. Alec recognized one of the tong holders – the man outside the hotel the previous evening. 'It hasn't taken them long to demote him back to the salt mines,' he thought.

101

He glanced at Kotaro – he knew now Kotaro had brought them here deliberately – another oriental subtlety? The pipe snaked away along the steel floor of the shed for three hundred yards or more, and Sally noticed that every so often along this length were posts set into the steel floor. At the far end of the floor was a large circular drum. As the pipe came along it was held by this drum momentarily while a circular saw sliced off exactly eight metres, which fitted into grooves around the slowly turning drum. As the drum filled up with eight-metre lengths, the pipe moved around the perimeter of the drum and was dropped at the far side into a large vat of water. The stench of sulphur and steam rose from this vat of water each time a new hot length of pipe was quenched in it. The cutting action on the drum was only momentary, but each check sent the red hot pipe twisting on the floor, dancing in a wild snake dance. All the men working on the site wore leather gaiters up to their knees, and leather-soled boots, but several times the pipe snaked waist high and the men lining the long path had to make a quick jump. This machine could make seven miles of pipe in four hours, pipe that was used for carrying electric wiring around buildings, conduit piping. Kotaro indicated a safe place for them to stand, on a platform overlooking the bending machines. Then he took out a cigarette and an amber cigarette holder. Into the cigarette holder he screwed a filter capsule. He put the cigarette holder in his mouth, absent-mindedly holding the cigarette in his hand, preoccupied with the sight before him. The man with the tongs had not looked in their direction. They had no sooner climbed on to the platform than the ribbon of white-hot steel coming out of the furnace jumped out of the first bending wheel. There was not an instant's delay. An immediate yell sprang up, everyone started to shout at once. The man on the machine pressed a button and a klaxon hooted. The man with the axe raised it in the air and with one blow severed the steel ribbon where it came out of the furnace. He stepped quickly to his right. The man behind him, holding the tongs, sprang forward and grasped the white hot ribbon in the tongs and began to run left down the length of the shed. He had not gone more than ten yards when a second man grabbed the ribbon in his tongs and ran after him, trying to keep the same distance from him. Where the ribbon of steel touched the ground, white hot sparks danced from it. A third man took over and then the fourth, the man who had followed Sally the previous evening. While they were running with this death-dealing dancing load, men cleared the bending machines and started to replace the broken former. Now ten men were running full tilt down the shed, carrying the steel with them. If they should stop, the steel stationary in the heating furnace would melt, and ruin the inside of the furnace. The steel had to be kept moving through that furnace at all costs. When the man at the front of the ribbon reached the post Sally had spotted, he turned round and started to run back again, passing in front of their observation platform with the steel ribbon caught round the post. The post obviously had ball bearings in it, since it spun round under the pull of the ribbon. The second man reached the post and ran round it, keeping in the path of the ribbon at the same distance from the man in front. Now fifteen men were running down the far side with the ribbon, and Sally could understand why so many men had been standing about in this shed when they came in.

She looked at Alec in total amazement, so inferno-like was the scene. Alec of course had seen such a plant before, knew the risks and the dangers, and had once taken part in a run when a bending former had broken. Now the man on the first bending machine had slotted in a new former, and they were ready to cut the ribbon back into the machines. A crane hanging from a gantry above his head rapidly lowered a long sliding shoe, which he kicked under the moving near-molten ribbon. The klaxon was still sounding but now he pressed another button and the note became intermittent, indicating to the runners, all of whom were now gasping with the heat and the exertion, that with luck their run would soon be over. The shoe started to rise to guide the ribbon back into the bending machines. This was the trickiest part of the operation. Each machine man waited with the jaws of his machine open to bite on the ribbon in sequence. It had to be done to an exact time, since if one machine closed before the ribbon had been bent by the previous machine, another former could be broken. Then the axe would descend again, and the second team take over.

At this moment, the fourth runner was level with the observation platform, in front of Alec, Sally and Kotaro. He had just passed them when suddenly he appeared to slip, and fell, sprawling on the red hot ribbon of steel. The steel was pulled beneath his body. He started a scream which could be heard above the noise of the klaxon and the men yelling. Two men ran forward to lift him off the ribbon of steel, burning its way through his chest, but then the fifth man was on him, fumbled getting his tongs off the ribbon of steel, the third man, still running, looked behind him when he felt the check on the ribbon and slowed down, incredulous. As he slowed, the ribbon whipped up into the air, and a slow snaking movement started along the ribbon between the third man and the fourth man still lying on the floor. Sally, horrified beyond belief, watched this loop in the coil travel forwards about six feet to where the man on the ground was rearing up, trying unsuccessfully to get to his feet. The loop snaked along the moving ribbon and wrapped itself around his neck,

104

a white hot collar of steel. Flames sprang from the steel as his flesh burned. The axeman saw what had happened, brought down his axe, and the second team grabbed the ribbon and started to run, round a post, at right angles to the first team, round another post and parallel to the first team but a safe twenty feet to the wide of them. When they got to the man lying on the floor, the ribbon of steel had burned through his throat.

Sally, watching it all happen, suddenly realized that one of the men lifting the body of the Japanese was Alec. She hadn't noticed that he had gone, so swiftly had he vaulted off the back of the platform and run down the lane to where the Japanese lay writhing. Unheedful of his feet, he kicked at the ribbon of steel and freed the Japanese from it. The runners had stopped as soon as the axeman cut through the steel the second time. They dropped the writhing ribbon on the ground, and clustered around the dead man. One brought a sack, and with it they wrapped the man's head and shoulders. Then four of them brought a piece of corrugated asbestos sheeting, laid the man on it, and carried him to the door of the shed. An ambulance was waiting there, called by the first hoot of the klaxon. Usually, it was a wasted journey – this time they bore a grisly load back to the Company hospital.

Alec came to the platform where they were still standing, Sally with her hand to her face, the memory of that burning figure etched on to her mind. Alec reached up and, before Kotaro could move, he snatched the amber cigarette holder from his mouth. Near the end of the holder, in the best position to be held by the teeth, was a small depression. Alec showed the cigarette holder to Sally. 'It's a carbon dioxide gun,' he said sombrely. 'Fires a needle of ice. The carbon dioxide is solid under pressure in that filter he screwed into the cigarette holder. When he bites the button concealed beneath this depression, the dioxide gas fires the needle of ice up to thirty feet!' He turned to Kotaro. 'In the body of the victim, the ice melts, doesn't it, Hitohori-san, leaving no trace. There would be just sufficient shock to cause the man to stumble, if he were running, with a ribbon of white hot steel in his hand!' He handed the holder back to Kotaro, who took it and slipped it in his pocket.

'An amusing fiction, Haig-san,' he said. 'Now shall we carry on with the tour?'

Sally was about to ask to be excused from the rest of the trip round the steel works, but Alec gripped her arm and said, 'Yes, shall we?' She felt terrible but determined to carry on. As they left the platform, with Alec insisting Kotaro go first, he turned to them. 'I wouldn't let your fictions run away with you, Haig-san,' he said. 'We don't want to frighten Miss Michaels, do we?'

They walked into the blast furnace shed at midday. Though Sally had worked in steel for some considerable time she had never been so close to the blast furnace. It was as tall as a six- or seven-storey building. The blast furnace itself was a circular structure about fifteen feet round, stretching right up the centre of the building. Attached to the column of the furnace were innumerable pipes and valves and spigots. The main platform of activity was about twenty feet above the bottom of the furnace, but below this was a skirt, in which runways had been cut, runways lined with fine sand. These runways stretched to the side of an apron, and below the apron, trucks were standing, waiting to receive the pig iron when it would be tapped white hot and molten from the bottom of the furnace. Above their heads was another skirt of runways – these, Kotaro explained to her, were for tapping off the excess slag. The gantry along which they walked took them right up to the furnace, to where the furnace master

106

stood with his assistants, reading the gauges which record the temperature of the inferno inside. Although three feet of insulation stood between them and the molten metal, the heat was more intense than anything Sally had ever experienced. She felt the sweat running down her body, down the insides of her thighs as they stood there with Kotaro explaining the tedious intricacies of the Japanese blast furnace techniques. Alec, who apparently had forgotten the incident in the pipe mill, asked many technical questions beyond her comprehension. Kotaro replied to them all without once referring to the furnace master, a tall man, taller than any Japanese she had ever seen. He was wearing baggy trousers and a tattered shirt. Around his ankles were the gaiters she had seen most of the men wearing, fastened with criss-cross straps up to his knees. On his feet he wore leather boots. The whole gantry and platform on which they were standing was covered in a fine dust which stuck to her hands every time she touched anything. She felt sweaty, sticky, dirty, still nauseated by what she had seen. When a klaxon sounded on the roof of the blast furnace, the furnace master approached Kotaro and spoke with him. Kotaro smiled, and waved him away.

'It's the time for the midday meal, but the furnace master offered to stay if he can be of any assistance. I gave him leave to go,' Kotaro explained. All the men on the platform jumped down the stairs nimbly, crossing the narrow plate bridges over the molten metal runways with caution. Soon the entire blast furnace shed appeared deserted, the bubbling monster before them rumbling with the weight of metal contained within, left entirely to its own devices.

'That's something we wouldn't let our men do!' Alec said. 'We have a rule never to leave the blast furnace untended, day or night.'

Kotaro shrugged his shoulders. 'They've finished the last blow,' he said. 'The furnace will be tapped immediately they come back from their midday meal. For the next hour or so, it can be left to stew quietly. No harm can come to it, unless someone pulls the lever to open the tapping doors.'

'What would happen then?' Sally asked.

'All the molten iron inside would drain out, along those runways, into those trucks waiting to receive it.' He pointed below the gantry on which they were standing, down on to the sand about ten feet below them. The runways were shaped like a pit, the only entrance the blast furnace doors above, the only exit the drop straight into the trucks below.

'Let's walk round the furnace,' he said. 'Then you can see the details of the oxygen feed system on the other side.'

They started to walk along the spider's web of gantries surrounding the blast furnace, along tiny bridges that linked the main threads of the walk-way. 'Watch these bridges,' he warned. 'They can become very slippery!'

'Like you!' Sally muttered beneath her breath.

Alec went first, ahead of Kotaro, with Sally bringing up a reluctant rear. Alec and Kotaro had just crossed one of the bridges, and Sally was standing in the middle of it, when suddenly, behind Alec's back, Kotaro's hand flashed downwards on the bridge support. A pin holding the bridge in position snapped free, and suddenly the whole bridge swung downwards, hinged at the back. Sally plunged straight downwards and fell into the pit on to the sand below. She screamed as she fell, but Alec turned too late to grab her. He came to the edge of the pit and looked down.

'Alec!' Sally called. 'The sand is hot!' The sand had not cooled down much since the last time the blast furnace had been tapped, and already she was hopping from foot to foot. Alec grabbed a balk of wood on the gantry and flung it down.

'Stand on that!' he called. Sweat was dripping down her face, already her clothing was wet through with it. Alec looked round and grabbed another balk of wood. She stood with one foot on each of them. Already the wood was beginning to smoke where it lay in the hot sand. Alec turned to Kotaro, who stared back at him inscrutably. He lifted his fist and punched it into the Japanese's face. He saw the blood spurt from Kotaro's nose. It was a futile gesture which only relieved his immediate anger. He knew Kotaro had staged this whole business to get rid of Sally in such a way that no blame could be attributed to him or to Mitziguchi. Within a minute she would be overcome by the heat and drop full length on to that hot sand. Once that happened, she wouldn't last five minutes.

He looked at the sides of the pit, smooth all the way up the ten feet. Then, quickly making up his mind, he vaulted the low rail separating this part of the gantry from the pit, and jumped down. The heat of the sand came to him as a violent blow. It seemed to penetrate immediately the soles of his shoes. Quickly he stepped on to the balks of wood, where the heat was less, but his added weight pushed the balks farther into the sand, and they began actively to smoulder. The acrid smell of the burning oak filled his nostrils. Sally began to cough. He looked down to where the runway fell away into the vats. Only an almost superhuman jump could clear the other lip of the vat. He might just be able to do it, but Sally wouldn't stand a chance. At the far end of the pit was the casing of the blast furnace with levers protruding from it. They were identical and each one had a prominent Japanese sign beside it. He cursed his inability to read Japanese. Some of those levers would cover tubes into which pyrometers and thermocopiles could be inserted into the hearth of the furnace. Others would control the tapping tuyères from which samples of the iron could be removed, about a pint at a time. But others would control the hydraulic opening of the main furnace doors themselves. Press the wrong lever, and five tons or more of molten metal would pour down upon them.

Sally's knees began to give way. 'Hold on,' he said, and wound her arms about his chest. 'Can you grip your left wrist with your right hand, and your right wrist with your left hand?' She nodded, and gripped around his back. His face was only inches from hers. 'Don't worry,' he said. 'We'll be out of here in no time.'

She nodded, believing him. Slowly he let his shoulders go backwards until they were pressed against the pit wall. Sally was now lying along him. The balk of wood shifted under his feet. He lifted one leg, and jammed his knee against the far side of the pit. Now Sally was lying along him with a leg on either side of his raised leg. He brought the other leg slowly up, testing the strength of his shoulder-knee hold on the walls of the pit, and then placed his other knee against the wall. Now he was holding not only his own weight, but the weight of the sagging body of Sally. He let his hands drop down from his shoulders until they too touched the wall, but quickly he pulled his hands off the wall. It was almost red hot. He reached his hands up behind her back. 'Sorry about this,' he said, but she was past caring as he grasped her thick denim blouse from behind, pulled it out of her trouser tops, and ripped it. The effort of ripping almost caused his shoulders to dislodge from the wall. But he managed to tear it into two pieces and wrap them, one round each hand. It was when he was looking at the wrapping over her bared shoulder that he realized she had not been wearing a brassière or a slip. She was now naked down to the waist. Sweat poured down the golden skin of her back and yet, curiously, her back was trembling.

110

'Don't be afraid,' he said. 'This is called chimneying – mountain climbers and Boy Scouts do it all the time!' He didn't add they didn't usually do it up red-hot rocks. Already the heat had penetrated his trousers at the knee, and he felt the pain of the burn. He knew, from climbing years, that chimneying rapidly numbs your knees and the hands, anaesthetizing any pain. He dropped his hands down behind him and pressed them against the walls of the pit. Then with a sudden jerk he took the weight on his hands, and moved his shoulders up the wall about nine inches. He moved one knee the same amount, the other knee, dropped his hands and moved his shoulders up again. He had not taken three 'steps' when his knees went numb and he could no longer feel the blistering heat. He was about three feet from the top, with Sally already unconscious on his chest, when suddenly he saw the face of Kotaro looking over the rim of the pit, just above his knees. He put his hands down behind him and hoisted his shoulder one more pace. Next time he would be able to get his hands over the rim of the pit on to the railings and they would be safe. He worked his shoulders up, his right knee, his left knee. Kotaro was now bending over the edge of the pit.

'I've been looking for a ladder but couldn't find one anywhere.'

'No, you bastard,' Alec thought. 'You'd make quite certain when you sent the men away to their meal break no ladders were left lying about.' The heat from the sand below came coursing up the sides of the pit to him. The pain in the small of his back had grown steadily more intense as he climbed, and now his body almost refused each command to move. He brought up first his right knee, then his left knee. Both were within twelve inches of the top of the pit. Kotaro bent over the edge, his hands circling Alec's legs. Alec saw what he intended to do. 'Don't touch my legs, you bloody fool!' he said. 'Don't try to lift them or you'll dislodge my shoulders.' But Kotaro smiled innocently at him. 'What did you say?' he asked, that idiotic grin on his face. 'I didn't quite understand.' At that moment his arms encircled Alec's legs and he pulled upwards. Alec felt his shoulders pulled from the wall of the pit, and then his and Sally's weight plummeted them down. As he felt his head begin to fall, he kicked upwards sharply with his right foot. There was a crunch of bone as it connected with the underside of Kotaro's jaw, and then a clunk as the back of Kotaro's head struck the iron railing of the gantry. Alec and Sally fell head first into the hot sand. He felt his hair begin to shrivel where it hit the sand and quickly jerked himself upright and stood on the smoking balk of timber, pulling Sally on with him. The naked upper part of her body was covered in the hot sand where it had stuck to her sweat. He brushed the hot sand from her as deftly as he could, cleansing her shoulders, back, breasts, nipples, so the sand could not burn into her. Already her torso was covered with red dots he knew could rapidly become scars on her smooth flesh. Some instinct must have jerked her into consciousness when he touched her breasts, but she stood there silent, incapable of modesty. He stood her on one balk of wood and lifted the other balk, smoking, out of the sand and threw it along the pit towards the furnace. Then he sprang from one balk to the other, held out his hands, and she stumbled across to him. He put her hands on his shoulders, since she was incapable of standing on her own, bent down and dragged the other balk nearer the furnace. When he looked up, the unconscious face of Kotaro was hanging over the side of the pit. Already the heat from the pit had turned it a bright red. 'Serve you right, you bastard,' Alec said, out loud.

112

Soon they were standing at the base of the furnace. To climb up the projecting levers looked deceptively simple, almost like walking up a ladder, but any one of those levers could be the key to an instant death, melted alive in a river of flaming iron. Even the sampling levers would discharge a pint of liquid iron that, at over nine hundred degrees Fahrenheit, would quickly disembowel him. He took off his tie and turned to Sally. He made a knot in each end of his tie and put her wrists into the knots. Then he turned his back to her and put his hands behind him under her arms. Her arms came over his shoulder and down to his sides, held there by the tie which now stretched across his back like the strap of a haversack. He shrugged his shoulders and hoisted her up on to his back. Now she could not fall, no matter what happened. Now it was all or nothing for both of them.

He looked intently at the surface of the furnace by the first handle, but he could distinguish no pattern other than the honeycomb of the furnace insulation. Nor could he see any drips of molten metal adhering to the insulation below any lever, to warn him. He stood to one side and put his hand on the lever. He looked intently at the Japanese calligraphy of the sign, trying to sense in its brushwork some hint of danger, some warning message. But the inscription yielded no secret to him, no warning. 'All or nothing,' he thought and grasped the lever firmly with his hand and pulled it downwards, ducking despite himself in the fearful anticipation of that running river of molten metal. Nothing happened. He pulled again, giving it more weight. It was like pulling the handle on a beer machine – though infinitely more deadly. It moved smoothly, revealing behind the hinge a hole one inch in diameter. The hole extended into the furnace and was designed for the insertion of a thermocopile, an industrial thermometer. Looking upwards, he could see twelve levers,

113

and reckoned he could get out by touching only four of them. But which four? This was number one. Anxiously he looked for the next lever. There was one about three feet above him that appeared exactly similar to the first. He climbed on to the first lever, holding Sally on his back. Standing beside the next lever he pulled gently down. It started to move. He studied the inscription. It appeared similar to the inscription of the lever on which he was standing, but then, all the inscriptions had been hand painted, and to his European eyes they all appeared similar, but no two looked exactly alike. The lever continued to come down. He continued to press slowly. When the lever had depressed until it was about fifteen degrees from the horizontal suddenly he encountered an added resistance. Cautiously, oh so cautiously, he increased the pressure, and suddenly the lever dropped another fifteen degrees until it stood out at right angles to the furnace. About six inches to the right of the lever a piece of the insulation swung back to reveal the end of a two-inch pipe. From this two-inch pipe came a sudden globule of white hot iron. Quickly he tried to push the lever back up, the acid of fear running into his mouth. But the lever would not move. The globule grew in size. The heat from it was intense and he felt his skin burn, and then suddenly the globule burst, like a chewing gum balloon, and ran out of the pipe end in a thin trickle on to the sand below. As it ran along the hot sand it came to the balk of wood on which he had stood. The balk of wood, already charred to tinder by the hot sand, burst into flame. He took the lever next to the one he had pulled, and wildly yanked it. It opened, revealing a thermocopile hole. He scrambled up from one lever to the next, his hands holding close beside the furnace, balancing the combined weights of himself and Sally on one leg. He thrust upwards with that leg and their bodies slid along the furnace, past

114

three levers he dared not even brush. He looked about him. 'Two to go,' he thought.

Sally moaned on his back. 'My arms are breaking,' she murmured. He turned his head round until he could look at her face, by his left shoulder blade. She lifted her face to his. He tried to kiss her, but his mouth couldn't reach. She hauled herself up on her arms until their faces and then their lips met briefly. Her lips tasted of soot and sweat. 'I'm sorry to be a burden,' she said.

'Many men would give a fortune to see you stripped to the waist!'

'Sexy,' she said, and slipped back into unconsciousness. He glanced across at Kotaro, still out. His face was now suffused with blood, red and purple. Sweat was running along his cheeks and a large blob of it had formed on the bloody end of his nose. The sight of Kotaro gave Alec a sudden burst of energy and courage, and he reached above him and grasped a lever. It opened. Nothing happened. He reached up and placed his foot on it and then slowly heaved himself up the side of the furnace. Now there remained only one more step and he would be in reach of the gantry. As he had mounted the face of the furnace, so it had grown progressively hotter, until it was now almost too hot to touch, despite its insulation. He must be approaching the discharge doors, the ceramic shields behind the plates that held back the molten metal. Once those plates were freed by the movement of the lever, the ceramic shield would swing upwards, and the molten metal pour from the furnaces. There were three levers from which he could choose. Again he sought inspiration from the Japanese writing, but he could learn nothing. As he turned about, examining the three levers, suddenly Sally gave a groan. He reached a hand behind him and felt where the uncontrolled swinging had forced her ribs against one of the levers beside his body. Where the lever had dug into her soft flesh, the blood had now begun to run. The three levers were level with his chest, nearly four feet above the one on which he was balanced so precariously.

'Which one?' he muttered. 'Which one?' tortured by the possible consequences of the wrong decision. Then, quickly he made up his mind, and grasped the lever to the left. It swung out. He felt rather than saw the rush of hot metal, twisted his body violently to the side, ramming Sally against the lever that had cut her ribs. She groaned again, but now the globule of white hot iron had formed and spat its thin spittle down upon him. Again he twisted violently, cramming Sally's body against the lever, but the molten metal was pouring out and down. He jerked his thigh aside too late to miss the metal which splashed about a tablespoonful on to the jacket at his thigh. The metal burned instantly through the cloth, through his skin into his flesh, searing its way towards the bone. There was a sudden stench of burning flesh, the pain exploded up his side and his mouth opened as he yelled in horrified agony. He reached up to the lever in the centre, anything, anything, to get out of the pain. It didn't yield and he put his foot on it and heaved up and sprang sideways on to the gantry. He swung himself over the gantry and reached behind him and grasped Sally's unconscious body, the blood running from a gash beneath her breast, and flung her violently over the gantry rail. As her legs swung sideways, like those of an inert doll, her shoe caught the lever to the left of the one they had used to get finally out of the pit. The belly of the blast furnace burst open, spilling out its tons of viscera in a stream of white hot metal and sparks. There was a sizzling sound and a roaring in his ears, and the bright glow from the metal burning into his face seared his eyeballs. He freed his shoulders from Sally's arms and the tie and

116

raced over the gantry, round the bridgeway, until he was standing beside Kotaro. His face was still down, over that river of sizzling metal. Alec dragged him back from the edge and half carried the inert body to the side of the gantry behind asbestos screens to shield him from the glare and the heat. He stripped Kotaro's coat from his shoulders and ran to Sally and draped it round her, shivering with shock. He carried her over to the asbestos screen and seated her on a bench. Near by was a large flask which he upended, poured the cooler liquid over her face and down her throat, splashing it over her shoulders and chest. She coughed and spluttered as she regained consciousness. He tipped the flask into his own parched mouth. The liquid ran cool down his throat, cool as ice-floes. But then the burn started.

'*Saké!*' he yelled. 'Bloody *saké*!' And then they both burst out laughing hysterically, with the sudden relief of the release from the charring death of a bath of molten metal.

They were still laughing and quite drunk on the *saké* when the furnace master came pounding back up the gantry.

# PHASE 22

Pamela was sitting alone in the pub when Joe Michaels came over and sat beside her. Never sit on his own when there was a woman present.

'Randy old devil,' Pamela thought. 'Hello, Joe,' she said. 'How are things going, then?'

Joe was instantly flattered by her friendliness. He took off his flat cap and set it down on the table top. Still had a good head of hair, and was mightily proud of it. 'Can't complain,' he said. 'What are you drinking?'

Frank Lester, in the snug, could see into the public bar where Pamela and Joe were sitting. Joe turned round and looked across at him. 'Isn't that Frank Lester in there?' he said.

'I wouldn't know, I'm sure,' she replied, her voice cold with lack of interest.

'Like that, is it!' Joe Michaels gave a chuckle. Catch 'em on the rebound – makes life even easier. 'Can't see a good-looking widow woman like you sitting on her own,' he said, his gallantry clumsy but unmistakable. Five pints and five gin-and-tonics later, Joe was sitting at her side of the table, his chair practically touching hers. The pub had filled in the meanwhile and no one could have heard what they were saying for the general hubbub.

Which was a good thing, since Joe had reached the boastful stage and was talking about the Free Society. 'Too much talk,' he said, his voice beginning to slur. 'What they need is a bit of action to liven them up. There's only one man around here who understands action,' he said, 'and that's me.' His hand was resting in her lap. He turned it and gripped her inner thigh under the table. 'Like a bit of action, do you, Pamela?'

'You're like the rest of 'em, Joe, all talk and never do anything.'

'Don't I just!' he said, anger swimming to the top of the beer in him. 'Well, who the hell do you suppose it was blew up the coke oven? Elwyn? Old windbag Elwyn?'

'Who was it, Joe?' she quietly asked.

'It was Joe Michaels, that's who it was.'

'How did you do it, Joe? With dynamite from the quarry?'

'Dead simple,' he said. 'No dynamite. I shut down the main flow valves and opened up the main gas valve. There was five thousand cubic feet of coal gas in that oven when they switched it on!' Joe got to his feet and picked up her glass. 'Let's have another drink,' he said, but he saw the crowd standing between him and the bar, and turned and looked at her. There was a sly look on his face, of avarice and desire. 'Too many people in here,' he said. 'Let's get a bottle of whisky at the off-licence, and take it and drink it at your place.'

'Now comes the tricky part,' she thought. She gathered together her handbag and her scarf and they went out of the pub together. Frank Lester saw them go, and he drank his drink and followed them out. When they were in the street she put her arm through Joe's and whispered in his ear. 'Bloody hell!' he shouted, and turned right down the road, leaving her standing. When he was out of sight Frank Lester stood beside her.

'Thank God you're here!' she said as they hurried in the

119

direction away from that taken by Joe. Frank had parked Alec Haig's car down the road a few hundred years, in case it was needed. As they got in the car he asked her, 'How did you manage to get rid of Joe so easily?'

'I told him I thought you'd given me a disease!' she said. 'I couldn't think of anything else!'

He burst out laughing. 'Why, you treacherous minx! That'll be all over the steel works tomorrow!'

'He did it,' she said gravely. 'The coke oven!'

'How?'

'He said something about leaving the main gas valve open when he'd shut down the flow valves. Does that make sense?'

'It does. With the main gas valve open, lighting the coke oven would be like lighting your own oven at home, when the gas had been switched on for five minutes. Only the explosion would be three thousand times greater!'

'The lousy bastard!' she said, and began to cry.

Joe was stumbling along the road, past the steel works. He'd chased his pints of beer at the bar with whisky, and was well under the weather. As he passed the main gate he waited for the locomotive to cross the street. The shunting line stretched right across the main road, at road level and though there were no gates, there were large red lights, operated by switches on the line. He was standing there beneath the red light when he felt someone put a hand on his shoulder. 'Don't turn round, Joe.' He recognized the voice. 'Turn right when the locomotive has come through, and walk down the path at the side of the tracks. I've got some instructions for you.' The locomotive rumbled back on its ceaseless run up and down the line, the red light went out, and Joe turned and walked down the path. When they had gone a hundred yards the voice said, 'This will do here, Joe.' He stopped. He was just about to turn around when suddenly he felt a stunning blow on the side of the back of his neck, just below his ear. He fell to the ground, pole-axed. The man who had hit him, dressed all in black, emptied the sand out of the sock he held swinging in his hand, and put the sock in his pocket. He took a half bottle of whisky out of his pocket, wiped all the finger-prints from it, opened it and pressed it into Joe's hand. Then he lifted the hand and the whisky, forced open Joe's mouth and poured as much of the whisky in as would go. He dragged Joe over, away from the path, so that Joe's neck was over the railway line. He could see the shunting locomotive start up the line towards him, and ducked up the slope and over the low stone wall edging the railway cut. The driver of the loco-motive was in one of those sour moods – everything was going wrong tonight. He'd had a row with his wife before he left to come to work, he'd forgotten to bring his sandwiches with him, and now the damned headlight had failed on his loco-motive. There was he, driving up and down the line, hardly able to see more than a foot in front of the locomotive. This was the time of evening to be careful, of course. Too many drunks about! He never even felt the bump as the locomotive cut off Joe's head.

The man in black left the wall, walked about fifty yards, and then entered the steel works by the main gate.

'Good night, sir,' the gate-man said.

# PHASE 23

They were sitting in the 'pulpit', three of them, above the bars of the rolling mill. The crane driver had brought a white-hot ingot and lowered it gently on to the end of the bars. It measured six feet long by three feet thick by three feet high. Solid steel, free from phosphorus. By the time they had finished passing it backwards and forwards through the mill it would be only four inches thick and four inches high, but almost five hundred feet long. It would pass backwards and forwards through the mill ten times.

The crane driver looked down at the three men in the pulpit, above the bars. 'Something going on!' he thought. 'The rolling mill manager in the pulpit at midnight!'

Beneath the slab of solid steel the gripper fingers moved up and started to slide forward along the bars. The steel ingot was held. The man in the driving seat of the pulpit set various levers in front of him, and engaged a gear lever set into the floor rather like the gear stick of a motor-car. The jaws of the rollers slowly closed, a gigantic wringing machine. The mill manager checked the figures on the dial against a sheet of paper marked 'confidential', and beckoned to the man in the driving seat. The ingot started to move forward, towards and below them. When it reached the rollers immediately beneath the pulpit there was a ringing sound as the steel hit, and then was drawn through the jaws. The steel hissed as it was dragged into another set of rollers set closer together, and another and

122

another. When it reached the far end of the four-hundred-yard-long rolling platform it measured only two feet thick. The man in the driving seat worked a control on the floor using his feet. Two enormous fingers came out of the space between two rolling bars, the ingot was gripped and turned on to its side. The driver kicked in a clutch, and all the rollers altered their distances apart, then the still white-hot ingot came down the rollers towards them, to be squeezed again. Now it measured two feet by two feet, but was thirteen feet long. There was a blast of white-hot heat in the pulpit as the ingot passed beneath them.

'You wouldn't think it possible, would you?' The driver, with all his experience of hot rolling, had never met any steel so ductile, so easy to roll. It had been a difficult task to balance the temperature of the ingot and the pressure and the speed of travel, but now these vital figures had all been worked out by the back-room boys, and rolling suddenly became simple. He passed the ingot backwards and forwards along the rolling platform with ease. Now the ingot was only red hot, and the blast of heat as it passed beneath the pulpit was bearable. Each time the ingot passed through, the mill manager called out the next setting of the rollers, the speed of traverse, from the confidential papers in his hand. These figures registered on the dials of the pulpit, hidden from all but the driver and his mate, the mill manager, and the eye of a closed circuit television camera set in the roof of the pulpit, and not even the mill manager knew about that!

A large lorry was parked on the steel works car park. It had collected a load of steel sheets for Steel Fabricators Ltd of Prestwick, but the driver did not feel like returning tonight. The back of the lorry was almost filled with his previous load, wrapped in a tarpaulin. Under the tarpaulin was a crate eight feet high, eight feet long, and the width of the lorry.

123

In it was a television receiver, and a videotape recorder. They were getting a good picture from that camera on the top of the pulpit, really, when you think of all the metal about. You could read the dials quite clearly on the monitor screen!

# PHASE 24

The room was filled with flowers in the International Hotel, when Alec and Sally awoke the following morning. As soon as the molten metal had started to pour, the furnace team knew something was wrong, and came running. It took very few minutes to get the steel works ambulance to the blast furnace, and they were taken to the sick bay. Apart from a certain reddening of his features which would pass for excessive sunburn, Kotaro Hitohori had suffered no extensive damage. Sally's torso was covered in small red blemishes, but the nurse assured her they would disappear rapidly. The cut over her ribs, she said, would leave no scar. Alec's burned thigh, however, caused him much pain, and had to be cleaned and bandaged. The Mitziguchi Steel Works doctor appeared well qualified, and did all that was necessary. Apart from an enormous pain when he tried to walk, Alec appeared to have suffered no real damage. 'You very rucky man!' the doctor said, searching his limited vocabulary.

Was it deliberate? Or was it, as Kotaro himself had said, all an accident? Certainly, he had thrown himself on the mercy of Alec and Sally, had offered to submit himself to a tribunal of the top management of Mitziguchi, and any independent investigation Alec wished carried out would be done immediately. Kotaro apologized for his hand hitting the bridge release pin. Apparently, sometimes when the steel was pouring, it became necessary to shift that bridge out of the way in a hurry, hence the quick release mechanism. He was stunned when Alec hit him – of course, he forgave Haig-san and wouldn't even have mentioned the fact, but it was because he was stunned that he tried to help by clasping his legs. If he had been in his right mind! And then, if Haig-san had not accidentally kicked him under the jaw, for which of course he instantly forgave him, he would have been able to tell him which lever was safe, and which not, and Haig-san and Miss Michaels could have stepped out of the pit very simply. It was all so convincing, all so completely plausible. Especially when he presented to Haig-san, with bows and teeth clicking and that curious sucking sound anxious Japanese make in their teeth, the amber cigarette holder, complete with a packet of filter capsules, none of which, apparently, contained compressed carbon dioxide or slivers of ice!

Almost as if by magic, Alec's treatment was no sooner completed than his suit was returned to him, sponged and pressed with the burn hole invisibly repaired. With it were a matched pair of Japanese ties, silk lined, like Sulka ties, and his shirt which had been washed and ironed. Sally was given a box, and in it was a Japanese kimono, embroidered in the Shishu-moyo embroidered pattern of the lucky trio of pine, bamboo, and plum. Alec grunted when he saw it, but then he recovered his humour at the sight of her soft loveliness in it, and explained the meaning of the traditional pattern to her. Damn the man Kotaro! There was a subtlety in everything he did. Plum for Sally, with a complexion like the blossom, bamboo for Hitohori, soft, pliant, but hard and unbreakable. And the lofty pine for Alec himself, the pine that snaps in the storm.

And now, here was the room full of flowers, Japanese

126

azaleas, white chrysanthemums, funeral flowers, as Alec called them, and delicate orchids.

'How is your, er, back?' he asked Sally. She blushed again at the memory. 'It's coming on well,' she said. 'They think the burns will disappear quite soon, and already they seem to be fading. They gave me an oil to rub on it.'

'I know,' he said. 'I can smell it!' She pouted at him. 'What I really meant to say, is that it has a beautiful perfume, like all the oils the Japanese use!'

'Is your thigh hurting you?' she asked, her voice full of commiseration.

'Not too much!' he said. The burn had been clean and the pain had died down to a dull throbbing.

Leisurely they ate breakfast together, of fruit, and Kellogg's corn flakes, and soft boiled eggs. The eggs were tiny in size, much smaller than anything Sally had ever seen, and to her surprise she ate three.

'No steel works today?' she asked.

'No steel works! Kotaro may have been speaking the truth about it being an accident, but I shall not give him the chance again!'

She saw a spasm of pain cross his face. 'You ought to be in bed,' she said.

When lunchtime came, she looked round the door of his bedroom. He was asleep. She was dressed in outdoor clothing, a skirt, a denim shirt, under which this day she wore a soft comforting body stocking, and a short suède jacket. On her feet she had stout brogue shoes. She beckoned to the waiter who came to serve them lunch to leave the room undisturbed, and went out, silently closing the door behind her.

# PHASE 25

'Where have you been, Sally?' Alec asked when she returned. He was dressed in pyjamas and a dressing-gown, his leg out stiff on a pile of cushions in front of the low sofa. Papers and files were spread about him and he had apparently been working while she had been out. On the sofa beside him was a telegram.

'Walking. Just walking about!'

'Who with?'

'No one, of course. Why do you ask?'

He ignored her question and picked up one of the folders. He opened it and started to read. 'At seven-thirty p.m. the suspect was observed in the bar in conversation with Kotaro Hitohori.'

'The suspect – is that me?'

'It's only a way of naming the person in a report.'

'Is it! Well, I, for one, don't particularly care for it!' Her voice was not angry – rather was it cool and icily composed. He turned to the second page. 'The suspect was followed from the International Hotel and observation started at six-fifteen p.m. This was on the evening before last evening – the evening before those strange events of yesterday that almost crippled me!'

'Almost killed us both, you mean! Anyway, that's beside the point. What is more to the point is that you've had me followed!'

128

'Every time you've left this hotel without me,' he said wearily, 'one of my men has been close by you!'

'Has followed me, you mean! How dare you . . .' He didn't let her finish the sentence, but gripped her arm. 'I'll tell you how I dare,' he said. 'These men are not amateurs, and you are, and I'll be damned if I'll see you engaging in a private vendetta against them. Leave all that sort of thing to me – I'm a professional at it!'

'You've been following me to protect me!' she said, the ghost of a smile on her face.

'Yes, I have,' he said. 'I've not been following you personally of course, but I've had a man always near you. At least until this afternoon. This afternoon, you escaped from my man. Look, Sally, this isn't a game of Stratego we're playing, you know, with counters you move across a board! This has already gone further than bribing a typist to let you know what orders your competitors are likely to get, or photographing fashion models so you can reproduce your opponent's designs for the mass market! Six men have been killed, and yesterday we two could have been killed – and this afternoon, you went out for five and a half hours and deliberately escaped from the man I had following you. Now he too is a professional! He's a very good man at his job of following people, that's why I assigned him to look after you, and no ordinary person could shake him off. So, if you're not an ordinary person, what the hell are you, and what was your connection with Kotaro Hitohori, with whom you were seen having a drink in a bar?'

'I've no idea what you're talking about,' she said. 'I didn't know you had a man following me, so how could I have shaken him off?'

'By the oldest dodge possible – so old, in fact, that he'd forgotten about it. You went into a hotel and went into the

129

ladies' cloakroom. You came out of the cloakroom. When he had gone to the front door of the hotel to wait for you, you doubled back and into the ladies' cloakroom again. This time, you came out of the back door. And don't deny it!'

She looked steadfastly at him. 'I'm not trying to deny it,' she said.

'Good. You may not know it, but Kotaro has also had you followed since the night you drank with him in the bar.'

That really shook her. Then, to his utter amazement she drew up the skirt she was wearing, up past her stocking tops. Finally, when she had his attention, she held her skirt still. He could see the bottom edge of her panties, and the clips of the suspender belt flat against her smooth sunburned thigh. She came closer. One of the suspenders was broken, and it had been secured with a pin.

'That's why I went into the cloakroom the first time,' she said. 'But I didn't fasten the pin properly, and had to go back in again. The pin was sticking in my leg.' She drew the suspender aside and showed him where the pin had pricked her. Then she looked up at him. 'Mr Hitohori called me on the telephone that first night after we got back from the works. He asked me to go downstairs as there was something he had forgotten to give you. When I got down there, he bought me a drink and I found it was just a ruse to get me on my own to ask me out to dinner. I refused. Thinking about it since then, I realize that he wanted to make certain I hadn't recognized him, from South Wales. He tried to pump me, to see if I had ever met him – he tried that old gag, "Haven't we met somewhere before" – and when I said I'd never been out of Wales except to go for a holiday on the Costa Brava, he said he had never been to Wales. And now you can stop looking at my thigh, because that is the end of that!'

She drew down her dress. He blinked. He had in fact been

130

staring at her thigh, mesmerized. The pin-prick, she couldn't have faked that. Unless she were an absolutely superb actress. Suddenly he believed her.

'Why did you suspect me?' she asked.

'It was your father who blew up the coke oven,' he said, touching the telegram with sorrow. 'He killed those four men! Now he's dead, murdered by the Japanese.'

Her eyes filled as she realized the horrible truth of what he was saying. The tears ran down her cheeks as she stood there, silent, tears of a most terrible inner anguish. He knew no way to console her. He got up from the sofa, clumsily, went through into his bedroom and shut the door. A half an hour passed before she tapped gently on the door, opened it and came in. He was lying stretched out on his bed, his hands behind his head. He tapped the bed beside him. She came over and sat down. He took her hand in his. 'I've booked you on a flight which leaves Haneda at eight in the morning,' he said. 'The Company plane will meet you at Copenhagen, and fly you to Cardiff Airport, and then the helicopter will take you home.' She nodded. Tears were still in her eyes, but they did not flow. 'The Company will take care of the funeral,' he said. 'And we shall put your mother on the pension list. It wasn't her fault.'

At the mention of her mother she started to sob again, but managed to stifle them. 'We weren't very close,' she said. 'He was always in trouble. Mother used to say he made a rod for his own back. And then, he was never faithful, and that hurt mother most of all. It sounds a horrible thing to say,' she said, 'but once we get over the shock we shan't be sorry to see him go. He's brought us all so much trouble.'

He picked up the telephone and ordered dinner to be sent up. She went and took a shower and together they ate dinner in their dressing-gowns. After dinner, they listened to the radio for a while, playing softly, but then the Schumann piano concerto was announced, in Japanese and English, and angrily he turned it off. 'I can't stand piano music,' he said, by way of excuse. She had been sitting silently for some time, contemplating him. His sudden action broke her trend of thought.

'You're a very curious man!' she said. 'You have strange likes and dislikes!' He had a sudden urge to tell her why he didn't like the sound of the piano, but then he thought it was ludicrous still to be bothered about the death of his wife that seemed to have happened so long ago.

'Tell me about yourself,' he asked.

'A potted biography?'

'No, not that. Not dates of schools and all that sort of thing. Tell me about you, now. Tell me what you think is important, what you want out of life, what you expect to happen to you?'

'That's a tall order,' she said. 'Made especially difficult by the last few days. All my life there've been walls of possibilities around me. I've learned not to want impossible things. But, since I got your telegram, all those walls have been knocked down. I could never have believed that one day I'd be sitting here in a Japanese hotel with a man as attractive as you, or that someone would have tried to kill me, or that I'd feel the same excitement I now feel about the future. That's what you have done for me, unwittingly I'm sure.'

'Oh, God!' he said, not entirely in jest.

'Oh, don't worry – I'm not going to lean on you. I know a man like you would hate that. I'm only telling you this to let you see how impossible it would be to predict my future, post-Haig!'

'There's a very strong streak in you,' he said. 'I imagine it comes from the Celtic blood?'

'That's strange. I thought you must have Welsh ancestry, because there's a streak of iron in you. Both Mr Kai and Mr Giovanni think you're an absolute bastard. As hard as iron. I wouldn't have told you that, but they also respect you very much – it's amazing to me, as a woman, to see how much men can respect other men – they're both very devoted to you!'

He was pleased, but tried not to show it. 'Don't just sit there purring inside!' she said. 'Tell me what *you* think is important? What is it they say – "how does a nice girl like you come to be doing a thing like this?"' Now he was forced to laugh.

'It seems important to me. Somebody has to do it and I believe I can do it well.'

'But what about the rest of life? I mean, my work in South Wales only occupies a small amount of my time. Of course, when I am at work it occupies all my mind, and often I think about the day after I get home – but it doesn't absorb me the way it seems to absorb you.'

'It can't be a job I can do part-time,' he said. 'Look – what men do with their ability is important. When a man takes a job he should put his back into it, no matter what that job may be. If he puts his back into it, and uses all his ability and his skill, he has a right to expect to make profit from the job. If he's on a weekly wage, he has a right to expect the funds will be there to pay that wage fifty-two weeks a year. A lot of companies have been ruined by industrial espionage, you know, and the men who worked for those companies were thrown out of work through no fault of their own. That's why I think my job is important!'

'Of course, the fact that you can go anywhere you like at any time, and live in permanent luxury when you get there, has nothing to do with it, I suppose,' she said teasingly.

133

'Sorry, was I being pompous?'

'Just a little bit!'

'Yes, I admit the luxury is a part of it. I like good things and couldn't be happy in a life in which I didn't have them. But it's very easy to let them take over if you're not careful. Many men have been ruined by developing a taste for luxury – without the resources to buy it. That's when they turn to cheating and stealing.'

'And industrial espionage.'

'Yes, that too. The most dangerous master of all is greed! Absolutely implacable. It eats into you like an acid.'

'Have you ever been hungry?' she asked. 'I mean, really hungry for a long time – not just temporarily hungry because you've missed a meal?'

'Hungry like the miners of South Wales?'

'Yes, like them?'

'No, I never have been.'

'I thought not. If you had you'd know that a lot of greed comes from persistent hunger. People who have once been hungry will do anything to avoid it again.'

'Even murder?'

She thought for a moment. 'Yes, I think, even murder!'

Though it was still early, she got up, and made her preparations to go to bed. He sat in the chair and watched her. Then she came across to where he sat, and brushed his forehead with her lips. 'Good night,' she said.

She left the door of her bedroom open. He sat in his dressing-gown, reading the reports from the listening station in an isolated barn near the steel works. They had been able to get within one mile of the transmitter in the electric light bulb, and reception was first class, loud and clear. After about an hour, he heard her call. He went through the darkened sitting-room into her bedroom, his leg, he noticed, consider-

134

ably eased by the day of rest. She was in bed with the lights out, revealed in the glow from the opened curtains at the window. He crossed over and sat beside her bed.

'You all right?'

'Yes,' she said. 'It's just that . . .'

'I know,' he said. 'You don't want to be alone, just now.'

'One thing. I know he deserved what happened to him, but promise me you'll go after the man who killed him.'

'I promise,' he said gravely. 'Now try to go to sleep.'

'Not yet,' she said. 'Lie down in the bed and talk to me.'

She pulled the blankets aside, shyly, and he got in beside her. The bed was comfortably warm, redolent of her own body odour, sweet and fresh. He felt an instant sense of companionship. 'Tell me about young Alec Haig,' she said. 'The young boy who learned to chimney on the mountains.' She wriggled down beside him. He put his arm beneath the pillow about her shoulders and she snuggled into his side, relaxed and comfortable. 'Tell me what you were like at my age.'

'I'm not that old,' he said.

Suddenly she sat part up in the bed and lifted her body. There was a soft rustle and then her nightgown appeared over the blankets. 'I've just remembered – I'm supposed to have my body rubbed, twice a day, with that oil!'

# PHASE 26

When Alec Haig kissed her at Haneda Airport and put her, dry-eyed, on to the polar flight for Copenhagen, on the sad journey that would end in a tiny cemetery in Wales, he had two driving ambitions. One to deny to the Mitziguchi Steel Works any advantage from the secrets they had stolen from his company – the other to find the man who had killed Evan Brannigan and Sally's father. He was quite convinced Joe Michaels would not have killed Brannigan in cold blood – just as he knew Michaels had not the intelligence to run the industrial espionage set-up in South Wales. Somewhere, in that steel works, was another man, a shadowy figure of more than average intelligence, a man with more than the Free Society on his mind. That was the man Alec meant to uncover.

They drove him into the barn in the back of an old lorry, filled with bales of cheap cotton. Once inside, he listened avidly to the receiving transistor radio. From time to time the tape recorder whirred as Kotaro, more than a mile away, spoke to one or other of his radio team – usually in Japanese. Katsuhiro translated rapidly, wound back the tape for re-recording if the message had not specific importance.

'You've missed nothing?' Alec inquired.

Katsuhiro looked as if he had slept beside the transistor. 'Nothing,' he replied.

'That's very strange,' Alec said. 'We've picked up no reaction whatsoever to the death of Michaels. Surely someone must have reported it.'

'They may have passed a written message over the desk. The microphone is in the bulb above Hitohori's head. It filters out the mechanical noises. We only get a transmission with the human voice – if he speaks or if someone speaks to him.'

'He would be bound to say something,' Alec insisted.

At that moment the tape recorder began to turn, and there came the sound over the transistor of someone talking rapidly to Kotaro, walking nearer to the microphone.

'Here it comes,' Katsuhiro said in a whisper. 'A report from South Wales, from Instecon South Wales.' He had a pencil in his hand and was writing rapid Japanese shorthand on the pad beside the receiver. 'M. killed locomotive accident – rolling mill settings follow, and now we're getting numbers. 1015, 3 seconds, 10,500 ft. pounds, by five, 36 to 24, 26 seconds, 998 . . .' he called out the figures as they came over the transistor, writing them down on the pad in shorthand. Suddenly Alec exclaimed. 'They're programming a hot rolling mill for phosphorus-free steel,' he said. 'Temperature of metal, rolling time to first roller, pressure of rollers, number of rollers, dimensions, rolling time back into reverse phase – with that information anyone can roll the new steel without work-hardening it and cracking it!'

His mind flew like a computer over the South Wales organization, and the instructions he had given for security. 'Only three people know that set of figures,' he said. 'Ianto Griffin who does the final calculations, the rolling mill manager, and the pulpit driver, and he's not supposed to see them, only to have them called out to him while he is actually rolling.'

The transistor had come to the end of the figures, which

were obviously being read from a telex message by the operator. Then came the remainder of the message. 'Urgently recommend you personally investigate rumours blast furnace programmation!'

'Whom do you know at the airport?' Alec asked quickly.

'Everyone,' Katsuhiro said. It was no boast. He'd made it his job to know everyone.

'Now listen to this,' Alec said, 'and think hard and fast. That polar flight doubtless took off on time – that could be forty minutes ago. Can you turn that plane back?'

Katsuhiro thought for a moment. 'I think I can do it,' he said.

'I have to get on it.'

While Katsuhiro raced to a telephone, the driver bundled Alec into the back of the cotton lorry, and drove him to the airport. At moments of crisis such as this Alec's mind became cold, his brain crystal clear. With a secret like the advance electronic programmation of the blast furnace to be gained, Kotaro himself would lose no time in coming to South Wales, probably on tomorrow's polar flight. By the southern routes, Alec had no hope of beating him back. He needed desperately those twenty-four hours.

He was in the bar when Katsuhiro joined him, with a catlike grin on his face. 'It has already started its return,' he said. 'Luckily it was late on take-off, and had been airborne only fifteen minutes. At this very moment, I imagine, they are fastening their seat belts, putting out their freshly lighted cigarettes, and grumbling like hell!'

Alec whistled in admiration. 'How did you do it?'

'My friend in Catering. He thinks the food put on board that plane before take-off may have been contaminated. He has had to warn the control tower to tell the pilot that no one must touch any of it – not even the coffee! They gave the pilot the alternative of continuing all the way to Copenhagen for fifteen hours without food or coffee with a cargo of hungry passengers, or of turning back. Very wisely, he decided to turn back!'

No one was more surprised than Sally when Alec, a late but lucky passenger, walked on to the plane. 'Somehow I'd already decided we had said good-bye,' she said, 'since everyone thought the plane was going to crash. They told us a cock-and-bull story about contaminated food – but everyone thinks the plane is due to fall apart. There was a man sitting next to me, across the aisle, an aeronautics expert, and he told me he could hear the engines were faulty even before we took off. He says . . .'

'I wouldn't pay too much attention to what he says, if I were you!'

# PHASE 27

There was deep snow on the ground when the helicopter bringing Alec and Sally from Cardiff Airport arrived at the steel works. Sally shivered in the cold air, but that wasn't entirely due to the sub-zero temperature. Immediately on arrival Alec put Sally into a car to take her home, instructed Sodaberg's secretary which flowers to order, and told the Personnel Officer himself discreetly to supervise all the funeral arrangements.

'It's a great expense,' Sodaberg grumbled. 'Company funeral, pension for the widow, and now flowers!'

'It can't have escaped you,' Alec replied, his voice dangerously quiet, 'that if we give Michaels a Company funeral no one will suspect we have any knowledge of his responsibility for the coke oven disaster. We're buying time,' he added. 'Time we urgently need.'

Then he called a meeting of the blast furnace managers and Samuel Reynolds. Iron ore is mixed with coke, lime and other materials and fed into the top of a blast furnace. The coke burns, generates intense heat, and extracts oxygen from the iron ore. Molten pig iron flows out of the bottom of the furnace. Mixing the ingredients is tricky, and depends on the chemist's analyses of the ores, the lime and the coke. In South Wales they had 'invented' a way to grade these materials, and a complex computer set-up would 'order' the shunting train to collect exactly the number of wagon-loads to ensure a pig iron of the correct composition. The computer itself actually worked the shunting points and drove the train, as well as tipping the loads into the top of the furnace, skimming off the slag, and tapping the furnace when the reduction of oxide to iron had been completed. A triumphant blend of all the necessary skills, it had taken years of research and experiment – the first step in a fully automated steel plant. It was a secret worth a hundred millions.

'When will you be ready to make the first run?' Alec asked.

'We're ready now,' Joe Morley said. 'We'd have made the run on this shift if we hadn't received your message from Japan. How you got here so soon beats me!'

'Where are the vulnerable security points?'

'I'll defer to Ianto on this,' Joe said, 'since he knows more than any other man about the whole project.' Ianto was of the new breed of steel men. A doctor of philosophy of Swansea University, his thesis had been on the subject of automated controls. Instecon brought him back from Pittsburgh when he became part of the brain drain, looking not for more money but more opportunity. They bought the finest available computer for him to experiment with, and gave him a salary that would have been the envy of every man in the steel works had they known its value, and that a half of it was paid in Switzerland into a numbered bank account, tax free. An ascetic man of simple personal tastes, he lived in lodgings at the Heads of the Valley pub. Some said Ianto never knew the time of day – certainly, he had no thought to spare for the ordinary preoccupations and human failings of man. His was the mind of a dedicated theoretician. Every day he completed the *Daily Telegraph* crossword puzzle in his head in four minutes. 'What on earth was five across?' they'd ask as he came into the staff room for lunch. And without referring to the newspaper he always knew the answer.

'Security is not something I've spent a lot of mental effort on,' he said mildly, his eyes blinking as he found himself the focus of attention, 'but you could repeat the whole process if you had three things. You don't need the memory tapes, since they merely record what's in the various wagons, and that obviously changes with each new batch of ore that comes in. You would need the programme, and that's on one tape, and could be copied. You would need the circuit drawings for the console, since the tape merely issues electrical instructions, and the console is wired to carry out those instructions.'

'Where would you find the drawings?'

'They're kept here, on these charts.'

On the wall was what seemed a shallow cupboard. He opened it – using a standard key, Alec noted – and disclosed charts mounted vertically, on arms which could be removed. Thus any electrician needing to service part of the console could take out the relevant chart and trace the wiring. He picked up the telephone and dialled the internal code for Sodaberg's secretary. When she came on the line he spoke to her in Swiss-German. 'Get on to Françoise immediately,' he instructed, 'and ask her to arrange for Toni to come here right away. Send the plane to Zürich for him – it's waiting in Cardiff. And tell her to tell him it's another Eisenbahn!'

Ianto smiled when he put down the telephone. '*Schweitzer-Deutsch, nicht wahr?* A fascinating corruption of *Hoch-deutsch*! And Eisenbahn, wasn't he the man who broke into the Louvre . . .' He saw the stony look on Alec's face, and hastily stopped. Alec cursed himself for forgetting the breadth of this man's knowledge.

'You'd also need the circuit drawings for the blast furnace connections – the thermocopiles, the electronic gas analysis circuits, and the readings when the furnace is actually under fire.'

142

'And they are kept where?'

'Here, in this cupboard. And the readings show upon these indicators, as well as being fed electronically to the computer tape.'

'So anyone who could get in here, could get all he wanted of the whole scheme?'

'He'd have a job,' Joe Morley said. 'There's always three men in here, day and night, seven days a week, and when they start running that programme, they won't have time to open the doors for anyone!'

Alec thought for a moment, his brain too whirling like a computer. Then: 'This is what I would like you to arrange,' he said. He spoke to Samuel Reynolds, the man in charge, deferring to him as men in the past had always deferred to the Old Man. Sam felt the blood stir again in veins made thick by forced retirement. There was a luminescent quality about this man Haig, Sam thought, a quality of leadership if you like, but something more than that, a quality of inspiration. Even Samuel Reynolds, predestined by blood lines as a leader of men, could feel it and warm to it.

'If we run the computer on the last shift tomorrow night, starting at twelve o'clock, how long should it take to run a load through?'

'Ten hours,' Sam replied, without need to refer to his managers.

'At ten o'clock in the morning, after we've run the load, could we have the electricians in here, and the heavy gang, and I would like that console stripped and moved out with all those charts and the computer tapes on to a lorry. We'll take it all to Cardiff – you can hire one of those security firms for the journey – and we'll put it on the plane and fly it to Zürich. Could all that be arranged?'

Sam Reynolds didn't argue. 'No difficulties,' he said.

143

Alec saw one. 'You can move back into your old office,' he said. 'I'll get Mr Sodaberg to move out.'

Sam turned to him and smiled. This was it, the challenge again, the chance to do a job, however small, and do it well. 'Whom do you want on duty tomorrow night to run through the programme?'

'Just a normal crew,' Alec said. 'No managers, no supervisors other than those normally on duty. See if they can run it through on their own.' He turned to Ianto. 'Above all, Ianto, I don't want you within a mile of the plant tomorrow night. Nor you, Mr Reynolds,' he added, smiling.

'What a pity! I was just starting to feel useful again.'

The managers gathered close around him, glad, if truth were known, to have his reassuring figure back at the helm. They had worked the computer through carefully, had selected a fine team of men, and had no doubts about the success of the overnight run – but it was comforting, reassuring, to have the Old Man back again.

'Where will you be if we should need you?' Sam asked.

'You won't need me,' Alec said. 'And anyway, I have to go up to London. I shall be back just after nine on the morning after tomorrow, when I should like nothing better than to see a load of pig iron, made by this lad here.' Affectionately he tapped the console. One of the high tension valves 'sang' as its anode resonated, as if to answer him.

'You have a valve needs changing there – why not use a PP37 transistor?' he said to Ianto, to pay him back for the *Schweizer-Deutsch*!

The news that they were to run the blast furnace on the computer the next night ran through the steel works like wildfire. They had run it before, to everyone's great interest, but there was an air of tension about this particular run, as if it signalled something extra special. The fact that they were to remove all the 'brain' to Zürich after the run added to this feeling – it was 'all or nothing', with no chance for a second run if things went wrong.

'That should bring Kotaro to South Wales,' Alec thought. Then he made arrangements for his journey to 'London'. The helicopter took him no farther than Chepstow, where he had his car waiting. Within two hours he was back inside the steel works, though no one saw him arrive.

# PHASE 28

Toni turned up from Zürich later that evening, in a post office van hired for him in London from a company specializing in that sort of thing for films and television. They can let you have any 'official' vehicle, from a police car with a whirling blue light to a fire engine. The post office service van was small, inconspicuous. Toni had been given the lay-out of the plant from Zürich, and drove around the perimeter road, familiarizing himself. Then he found the switchboard, and started the 'annual maintenance'. When he had cleaned the switchboard, he found two faults – one was in the private office Alec was using. It took only a few minutes to repair that one. The other was in the computer control room of the blast furnace. When the girl on the switchboard tried to ring them to tell them he was coming, the circuit buzzed and hummed so much she could hardly make herself heard. When he got there, they were waiting for him. The fault, as he soon discovered, was in a transformer box, and a junction box. He had spare parts in the van, and luckily the replacement took only an hour. By ten o'clock, the telephones were working perfectly again, and he went back to the switchboard. The switchboard girls had just brewed a cup of tea, since they couldn't be spared on nights to go to the canteen, and he sat drinking with them for several minutes.

'What a nice man, for a foreigner,' they said as he left.

'I'll just pop into that Mr Haig's room to make certain his

146

phone is all right,' he said. When he got there he opened his large green leather tool bag and took from it three boxes, small enough to carry telephone instruments. He placed them on a table, out of sight of the door, and plugged one of them into the mains. He wired from that one to the other two. From the top of the two cardboard boxes he pulled telescopic rods vertically about three feet, and let down the sides of the boxes. Inside was a television screen about five inches by four inches. On the screen could be seen the interior of the computer control room, photographed by the two closed-circuit television cameras he had installed in the telephone transformer and junction box he had just replaced. Toni had once used this same system in an invention to catch an art thief, Eisenbahn, in the Louvre. No one could move in that control room without being seen on the screens in Alec's office.

Alec himself had spent his day, as he spent the first day in the steel works, in innocent conversation. Frank Lester had taken the day off, and had spent it in the pubs and the clubs. Pamela, after an initial protest from Alec at her involvement, had spent the day in the shops and the two supermarkets the steel town boasted, and had had her hair washed and set three times. Now they were all in Alec's room in the Rhyd Hotel, sifting through the bits of information they could recall.

'Whoever killed Joe Michaels must have come into that pub at some time or another during that evening. He would come in on his own, and he would leave on his own immediately after Joe Michaels left with Pamela, and before you, Frank, followed them. If he had seen you with Pamela, he would have guessed something was wrong, and nothing would have made him go near Joe that night.'

'Also,' Pamela said, 'it's someone who knows the workings

of the steel works very well. I didn't know the locomotive was working as late as that!'

'It's also someone who had the opportunity to knock out the headlight on the loco – remember that!'

There was a knock on the door, and Sally came in. Alec had not seen her since the morning when he put her into the car, but her face was drawn with worry. She was grateful for the way the Company was helping. 'It would have put Mother into her grave to have to cope with all that,' she said.

Alec apologized for asking her to come out of the house at a time like this. 'I wouldn't have done it,' he said, 'but you may have the one piece of information that is vital to us.'

She sat down and he poured out a drink for her.

'What do you want to know?' she asked, composed.

'Did your father have any unusual friends?' he asked. 'Anyone at all of whom you'd say, fancy him being friendly with my father? Someone you may have glimpsed him with on the street, who may have come to the house, anything.'

She sat there and thought. 'Recently?' she asked.

'Yes, particularly recently, though it might be helpful to know about anyone, say, six months ago, before all this business blew up and they doubtless started precautions not to be seen together.'

Alec was doodling on a piece of paper while giving her time to think. From the many conversations he had held that day, a few names came to him, and he wrote them down. Then, one by one, he crossed them off again, leaving only one. He was staring at that name, when suddenly Sally spoke it.

'Peter Reynolds,' she said. 'They seemed such poles apart. I haven't seen them together for a long time now, at least a couple of months, but I saw them together a couple of times, in that old quarry back of Brynfyn. Thick as thieves they were!'

'And they didn't see you?'

Pamela laughed! Sally blushed. 'Hardly likely, is it?' Pamela said, still smiling. 'The old quarry back of Brynfyn is where you go to do a bit of courting – if you have a gentleman friend with a motor car!'

'Peter Reynolds took Dad up there in his car!'

'Ah, yes, but that wasn't for courting, it seems!'

Alec crushed the paper he held in his hand. From the list of people entering the steel works that evening, as remembered by the gate-man, only one man had come in after Joe Michaels had left Pamela. The night shift started work at ten o'clock, so none of the night shift men could have been Joe's assailant. But Peter Reynolds had walked into the steel works, about twenty-five minutes after Pamela had got rid of Joe – time enough to walk up the side of the locomotive track and back again. Peter Reynolds lived with his father, in the Company house, inside the main steel works gates.

Frank had been deep in thought.

'Peter Reynolds came into the pub. I'd forgotten him, because he didn't stay for a drink. He came up to the bar, looked round, and then bought a packet of cigarettes, and left immediately. I remember now because I heard the landlord say, "We sell drink too, you know!" He doesn't like them going in there just for a packet of cigarettes.'

'Good man,' Alec said. 'This is all circumstantial, of course, but can you remember what he looked like?'

'I can't remember much about him,' Frank said, deep in concentration ' – he was in and out in a flash. But I do remember he was wearing a dark suit – yes, now you come to ask me, he was all in black.'

# PHASE 29

Alec was all set by the time eleven o'clock came on the following night. The local Army commander, Major Robinson-Waly, had been delighted with Samuel Reynolds's suggestion that his trainees should mount an exercise within the steel works. 'Teach them street fighting?' Samuel suggested. The officers, too, were delighted, since Sam's hospitality was legendary and the headquarters was to be set up in Sam's dining-room. 'I suggest we have two companies, that's about two hundred men, with rifles loaded with blanks. I shall come along myself – thank you for your kind invitation to take dinner with you – and bring a captain and six subalterns.'

Mrs Reynolds engaged outside help to assist Annie with the serving – a widow woman called Pamela who lived by the back gate.

The soldiers arrived in the steel works about five o'clock in the afternoon, under the command of the subalterns who took them in demonstrations of street fighting in and around the rolling mill, the Bessemers, the strip mill and the blast furnace. Dinner was long and protracted. The men were allowed to occupy the daytime canteen and its adjacent sports room of the social club for the two hours from eight o'clock until ten o'clock, when a series of night manœuvres was to start. Peter, at first sceptical when he heard what was to take place, had no reason to suspect his secret was known, and began to

150

welcome the diversion. The army detachment was so obviously dedicated to the maximum of running about and noise that he realized they would make a helpful cover for his nocturnal activities. He asked to be excused from the dinner table about ten o'clock. 'Got a young lady!' he confided to Major Robinson-Waly, who nodded in alcoholic agreement. As Peter left the dining-room to go to his room, Pamela, who had just served more coffee, drew aside the curtain and opened the window. Frank saw the signal and knew Peter Reynolds would soon be leaving the house. After a few minutes, he saw him slip inconspicuously out of the side door, dressed entirely in black, a black suit, with a black polo-necked sweater. Frank began to follow him discreetly down the path that led to the works and eventually the blast furnace control room. 'Don't get close to him,' Alec Haig had said, most emphatically. 'Your purpose there is merely to let us know when he leaves.'

Alec had moved the television receivers out of his office into the quality control room in a separate building behind the blast furnace. The room was warm, in contrast to the outside, where the temperature had been four degrees below freezing all day. Theodore Charalambous Pappayannikas, known as Toni, felt the cold worse than Alec did. 'It is colder than this in Zürich in winter,' Alec teased as Toni crouched over the stove in the corner of the room. 'Yes,' Toni said. 'But it's a still dry cold, not this biting wind you get here whistling around the buildings.' The snow that had been on the ground when Alec and Sally returned from Tokyo had now thickened – each slag heap a miniature Mount Fuji. Now the cold had really set in, and already they were having trouble in the works with frozen pipes. The continuous overhead railway carrying tubs of slag up the mountain side to the tip where Frank had worked had long streamers of ice hanging from the steel wire ropes and the bottom of the slag tubs. This late at night, most of the slag tubs were going back half empty, their mournful clank clank as they passed the suspension towers echoing against the softer roar of the blast furnace and the Bessemers. In front of Alec, on the desk, was an army radio, on net with radios carried by the operators of each platoon. An army radio had been supplied, also, for Frank Lester. The television system was working perfectly, and Alec could watch every move the operators made, as they prepared to run the load through the blast furnace entirely controlled by computer. 'It's like these blind landing systems they have on aircraft,' Alec said to Toni. Toni was lost in the world of computers, his speciality mechanical, radio and television. He could make a metal object do almost anything – guns that would fire hypodermic needles, hydraulic jemmies that would force open the doors of strongrooms, television cameras that could be concealed anywhere, microphone transmitters that could bug a small room or pick up the sound of the human voice at a distance of a quarter of a mile. He had made the electric bulb microphone Antonio Giovanni had brought to Japan.

He came from the stove and went to look out of the window. The icicles had grown at the corners of the frame when cautiously he drew the curtains aside. Alec was sitting before the television screens, watching intently every movement made in the control room. 'Think of it,' he said to Toni and the Captain of A. Company. 'There's a vast fortune in effort and expense locked up in that one room. Anyone can walk in there and steal it, and there's not a thing we can do about it.'

'Can't you charge them in the courts?' the Captain asked.

'Charge them with what? Breaking and entering? Stealing a

few pieces of paper and a computer tape costing twenty pounds at most? It's not the cost of the materials they take that bothers us – it's the hidden value of all the work that's gone into it. At law a piece of paper is a piece of paper, though the hieroglyphics on it could be worth a million to any rival concern. Take a secretary – goes home with the location of the key to the filing cabinet – a harmless secret, or so you might think. Knowing where that tiny key is could make all the difference to an industrial spy, breaking into premises during the night with a loaded camera and four pages of facts to photograph in a hurry between the night watchman's rounds. If you catch the agent, you can at least charge him with breaking and entering – but how do you charge the silly girl who has a lager-and-lime too many? Some of these agents are trained industrial psychologists, you know. They have to be. Give them ten minutes with a sales manager at a conference, a harmless conversation over a couple of gins in the bar, and before he knows what he's doing, the sales manager is unbuttoning his woes, confiding in the very man who's out to kick the company from under his feet!'

'I think our method on active service of sticking spies up against a wall and shooting them is much more effective!' the Captain said.

'I'm sometimes tempted to think the same,' Alec replied, his eyes never leaving the television monitors. 'But then, we hire at an enormous salary increase a man who has a successful record with another company, and you know, the first thing we do when he comes to work for us is to pick his brains clean, to uncover everything he knows about his previous company's operation. There are companies which hire men just for that brain-picking session, and then post them to some sinecure where they can't do the same damage again. Some firms even hire men, interrogate them, and then take the first opportunity to fire them. It's a rotten game.'

Toni had come back from the window, and sat himself at the table. On the table were a couple of bottles of wine. He poured a glass, and drank deep. 'You could always come and work with me in my little garage above Zürich, Alec!' he said jokingly, for he knew his man.

'It would kill me!' Alec said. 'Working for a big company is like being in a private army – you develop a "big company feeling". The company becomes father and mother to you, yes, and wife too sometimes!' He fell silent. Toni knew the story of Alec's wife from Jacques de Blaie. There was nothing ever that he could say. Only rarely did he see these lines etched into Alec's face, but they came from deep well springs of black misery he knew would always drive Alec on and on. Usually they came just as a particular job was nearing its climax – often when the name of the hidden agent or his contact had been discovered and one started to ask 'Why, why did he do it?' Toni knew that, more than anything, it was the bitter disappointment in humankind, the fallibility of avaricious or over-ambitious people, with no sense of values other than a greed, a lust, an insatiable appetite for personal gain or vengeance. This was what brought the lines to Alec's face, this and the knowledge that there was no single person, now Marika was dead, with whom Alec could link hands and leave behind the horror of it all. There's no misery so bad as one you cannot share.

Alec stirred uneasily in his chair as the radio set began to crackle with a message from Frank Lester. 'He's just left the house,' Frank said, 'heading down the path towards the works.'

'Whatever you do, Frank, don't let him see you, or the

154

whole business will be ruined. I'd prefer you to lose him than have him spot you.'

'I understand,' Frank said.

The Captain had not taken dinner in the house but had shared a cold supper with Alec and Toni – true it had been a sandwich of cold breast of pheasant, and they had washed it down with a bottle of Moselle, a Kaseler Timpert Templer-herrenberg Spätlese of 'fifty-nine that Samuel Reynolds had shipped to him from his old vintner in Devizes, Wiltshire. The Captain was pleased to have avoided dinner, finding Alec Haig, with his fund of international stories, a much more stimulating companion. He had been fully briefed about this exercise. The issues to him were simple – our side, their side, black and white, right and wrong. He knew there was an enemy agent and a 'Britisher' who'd gone wrong, and he was eager to see them brought to justice.

'Not too eager,' Alec said. 'Keep all your men and officers under cover until we see the two men on that television screen. When we see them, I want your men placed quietly around the blast furnace in sight of each other!'

'There'll be no shooting from the enemy?' The Captain had sounded disappointed. 'No,' Alec insisted. 'There'll be no shooting.' He knew his men too well. 'There might be a bit of a rough house!' he warned. 'Jolly good,' the Captain said, his eyes glowing. 'Our lads are good at the old unarmed combat!'

Now Peter Reynolds was on his way. Somewhere Kotaro Hitohori was also in the vicinity. Ole Neesgaard of Instecon Copenhagen had watched him land in Copenhagen off the polar plane twenty-four hours after the flight Alec had taken. But from Copenhagen they lost track of him. He had plenty of time to reach the valleys by any one of a hundred routes.

Suddenly there came another signal from Frank Lester.

'I've lost him!' he said quietly. 'He didn't come down the main road into the factory!'

Alec cursed quietly, but his voice was calm as he spoke into the microphone. 'All right,' he said. 'Don't worry. But make certain you don't stumble into him. Get yourself into the centre of the road – after hiding that radio somewhere, and come down here, making as much noise as you like.'

'It's damn cold out here!' Frank said.

'Never mind – we've got a fire waiting for you. One thing, though, when you get here, don't come near the quality check room until you can be absolutely certain no one is watching you.'

Eleven o'clock passed, then eleven-thirty. The atmosphere in the quality check room grew more and more tense. Then came the time to start the computer control. Exactly at twelve o'clock, Alec saw the computer assistant, sitting down at the console, start the feed of the programmer tape. On the programme were specific instructions – the computer was telling the blast furnace and all its components what it wanted it to do. 'Cool down the furnace,' the computer effectively said, and the electronic mechanism opened the valves to allow cold water to flow in the furnace cooling pipes. This was one of the first of a thousand instructions to be given by the computer and instantly obeyed. This run, they were to manufacture steel for an order of over ten thousand tons for a Post Office tower in Malagasey, an order they had managed to preserve despite the Japanese price-cutting competition. The order specified no-phosphorus, and Alec knew that Instecon would have to pay a hefty penalty if any phosphorus were found in the finished steel girders. The computer worked out the loading for the blast furnace, calculated the amount of ore, coke, lime and other materials, worked out which truck loads of ore would add up to the exact chemical composition

156

required, and sent the shunting train into the ore sidings to pick up those wagons. The points were set on the railway, wagons came rumbling up to the base of the blast furnace tower, one after the other, to be tipped into the hopper at the furnace top, over three hundred and twenty feet in the air. Meanwhile, the computer worked out the dilution of the oxygen it would feed into the bottom of the blast furnace through the blow pipes, the amount of water, the oil/coal dust mixture that would be fed in simultaneously to ensure rapid burning of the ore. It had worked out all these details within one second, fed the information on to soldier tapes, which would actually see each operation through, adjusting where necessary, altering, reducing, increasing as information was fed back from the blast furnace instruments reading pressures and temperatures. All this information was stored on to the master tape, which flicked idly along from spool to spool on the computer facia board.

With the computer assistant was the electronics maintenance man, standing by for any fault in the workings of the computer. All circuits were triplicated – if any part of the system failed, the computer would mutilate itself, cutting off the faulty arm and replacing it instantly with a new and faultless one. The maintenance man stood by, just in case. Next to him on the console was the blast furnace shift manager – truth to tell, out of his depth! He was more at home on the spiderways and gantries, sensing the humming of the great vertical cylindrical monster, hearing the hiss and sizzle of the liquids and gases going in, the ores and liquid metal running down. Seeing the molten globules coming out of the sampling tuyères, smelling the sulphur on them, feeling the heat from them. Heat to him was a tangible thing. He knew if a furnace was 'running cold' or 'running hot' – the difference could be no more than a degree Fahrenheit, but it would reveal itself to him, and he would walk across to the complicated arrangement of valves and pipework and adjust a handwheel there, a lever here, until he could feel the furnace 'running right'. Here in the computer control room he had far more information. He had thermostats at every stage of the way down the long furnace – could see with his own eyes if the metal were running hot or running cold, but that didn't compare with the feel of the steel plates beneath his feet, the cold wind rising through the gantries, the blazing hot heat from the molten metal and the sand of the runways below.

The computer had achieved a complete programme by five minutes past twelve, with the blast furnace already charged and firing its first load, the soldier tapes standing by ready to marshal other wagon-loads as required. Ore and lime were already in the top of the furnace, burning down through the cleaning charges put in that afternoon to scour the furnace for the Malagasey order. The shift manager lit his first cigarette and sat back, his eyes never leaving the temperature gauges in front of him.

It was at that very moment that Alec, watching them on the closed-circuit television, saw them all go to sleep. Each one of them just nodded his head and went quietly to sleep. There was no sound over the listening network other than the click of the computer tapes and the hum of the air conditioning system. The Captain glanced at Alec Haig, then looked away quickly. 'Don't want to make a point,' he said, 'but you wouldn't catch chaps asleep on watch in my unit!'

'Call up your men and get them to stand by.' Camera two in the set-up was showing the reverse of camera one, including the doorway. After five minutes of no activity whatsoever, suddenly the door opened. Alec saw Peter Reynolds and Kotaro Hitohori. They opened the door and came through it quickly, locking the door behind them with a key which Peter put back into his pocket. Kotaro, surprisingly, carried a cane. He held the cane up in the air and then looked at its end.

'Nerve gas in the air ducts,' Alec said, and snapped his fingers. 'They're either unconscious for twenty minutes, after which time they'll wake up and never know they've been asleep, or, they're dead! He's testing for it with that cane.'

The Captain swallowed hard, that pheasant sandwich close to the surface.

'I don't think it would be the killer,' Alec said. 'They came in too confidently.' He was watching Peter and Kotaro carefully, his eyes flicking from camera to camera. Kotaro was studying the computer mechanism, registering the various readings. He went to the wall cabinet, left unlocked, took down the plans and looked hastily at them. Then he found the master circuit, the one he wanted, and was able to run quickly through the computer set-up of master and soldiers, programmer and memories. The programmer and the memories he ignored. He ignored the soldier tapes, but seized on the master. He pressed a button on the console and the master tape wound itself back at high speed. He went to the cupboard where the tapes were kept in their eight-inch by eight-inch by one-inch boxes, and selected a tape. This he installed on the spools of the tape reader in the place of the one he had removed. Back at the console he wound the tape rapidly through until it was at approximately the same place as when they had entered. He took the charts from the wall and spread them out on the table beside the console. At no time did he pay any attention to the three men sitting at the console. He knew quite well what the gas had done.

'Move your men in,' Alec said to the Captain. 'A tight

ring all round the blast furnace. Make certain every man can see his neighbours, no ground left defilade between any two of them.'

The Captain issued his instructions.

At that moment, Alec, Kotaro and Peter Reynolds heard the tap on the control room door. There were no windows looking into the control room. Kotaro beckoned for Peter to remain silent and then, cool as a lemon ice, he unscrewed a cap from the top of his cane. From the inside of the cane he produced a roll of paper, rice thin. He spread the sheets, one by one, under the charts from the wall cabinet. When he had covered a sheet of rice paper with a chart, he held the stick in the air above the centre of the chart, about three feet away, and pressed a knob on the stick. There was a blaze of incandescent light in the room which set the closed circuit television camera limiters buzzing. The picture bounced up and down several times after each shot, but when Kotaro had finished he had, on rice paper, a perfect reproduction of each of the charts. He rolled up the rice paper and put it back into his cane. The knock on the door had not been repeated – Alec remembered the meeting with Samuel Reynolds and Joe Morley who had said that, once the men were running a programme, they would not have the time to answer the door, let alone open it. This must have been one of the men from the platform of the furnace, who'd never know how close he'd come. At the sound of the knock Peter had drawn a wicked-looking commando knife from his trouser seam. The whole operation in the control room took ten minutes, then Kotaro and Peter Reynolds opened the door and left as quickly as they had arrived. It was apparent now why Kotaro had been sent for – only he had the breadth of knowledge to sum up that room in one glance, and to know which was the vital information. With that master tape he could facsimile the entire

160

furnace operation, since, within five minutes, the computer had programmed itself to work for the next ten hours. On that tape would be every possible variation of furnace temperature, gas pressure, ore composition, and the exact method of dealing with any variation. It was like seeing a chess game written in advance, with every move your partner could possibly make plotted out, move by move, and, written beside it, every counter-move you would have to make to be certain of winning the game. It was a brilliant piece of programming of which Ianto was justly proud. And now, Kotaro Hitohori and Mitziguchi had the entire knowledge at their finger tips it had taken Instecon and Ianto so much effort to prepare.

Suddenly, the inaction was too much for Alec. 'I'm going in through your ring of men,' he said to the Captain, 'but no one, absolutely no one, comes out. Understand?'

The Captain was already speaking on the radio to his wireless operators. Alec left the quality control shed. Frank was waiting in the lee of the shed, blowing his fingers against the extreme cold. 'I couldn't be certain no one could see me,' he said.

'Do you like a fight?' Alec asked.

'What Welshman doesn't?'

'Then come with me. You can tackle Peter Reynolds, if it comes to a showdown, but leave the Japanese bastard to me. I have a score to settle with him,' he said, feeling again the throb of pain in his thigh where the molten metal had burned.

They crossed the floor of the blast furnace at a walking-running pace, and mounted the stairs to the ore loading platform. Along one side of the blast furnace shed, a walkway led only to one place, Computer Control, and the surrounding store rooms. They walked quickly along the high catwalk, looking down on the blast furnace itself rumbling away below them under perfect control.

At that moment the Captain, watching on television, saw the blast furnace shift manager wake up. Perhaps his constitution was more used to noxious fumes than that of his colleagues. Once awake, he looked around him guiltily and started to stare again at the dials in front of him. The maintenance man and the computer operator came awake at the same time.

'Is the air conditioning working?' the operator asked. 'For a moment I almost dropped off!' Not one of them realized they had all been asleep for at least fifteen minutes.

Alec slowed down as he approached the first store rooms outside Computer Control, built in the event of computer expansion. Sometimes, he knew, blast furnace men slipped up here when things were quiet. He entered the first room slowly, carefully. There was no one inside. He tried the handle of the second. It was unlocked. He opened it and went quickly inside. A shadowy figure moved on a chair facing the wall. He walked over to the chair. From it a man rose, one who worked on the furnace. He was about to explain his presence when Alec reached forward and put his hand over the man's mouth. He drew the man towards him, guided him to the door. He held a finger over his own mouth to indicate silence, opened the door and pushed the man through. The man gone, he slammed the door shut, dashed on tiptoe and stood behind the door on the far side of the room, Frank Lester behind him. Within a minute the door knob turned and the door started to open. He let the door open fully, partly concealing him and Frank. Peter Reynolds and Kotaro Hitohori came through the door, suspecting nothing. Kotaro was carrying his cane and the box containing the computer tape. 'Thank God he's gone,' Peter

Reynolds said. 'I thought he was going to stay there all night!'

'A crafty drag – is that not what a stolen cigarette is called in your slang?' Kotaro asked. At that moment Alec banged the door shut behind them, and they spun round. Kotaro's slit-like eyes closed even farther when he saw Alec, and he hissed between his teeth. Peter Reynolds cursed and drew out his knife. Alec kicked into the air and there was a snapping sound as his foot made contact with Peter's wrist. Frank had moved slightly to the side as the knife came out, and now he swung forward, his feet apart, his shoulder down. The roundhouse power-drive blow took Peter Reynolds in the stomach. He bent over and fell to the ground. Kotaro danced back, held the cane out in front of him, in the end a sword point, about ten inches long. It was pointed straight at Alec's throat. Kotaro beckoned with his other arm to Frank Lester. 'Over there,' he said, indicating the far wall, 'and lie down on the floor.'

Frank looked at Alec, who signalled to do as he was told. He went over and lay on the floor, his knee bunched under him, ready for a quick jump should the occasion present itself. Alec's eyes didn't leave Kotaro's face. Neither spoke. The tip of the sword blade in the end of Kotaro's cane weaved round in a tight circle. Alec spread his arms wide. Kotaro's stance said he was an expert fencer, but time was on Alec's side, Kotaro being compelled to move quickly. When it came it was a classic fencing movement, the stick weaving so rapidly Alec could hardly follow it. One two three, steps forward each time, Alec falling back, suddenly the point of the sword flicked forward, at his throat. He moved his head to the right, brought in his right arm sweeping in a semi-circle, downwards and inwards, upwards and outwards. He felt the tip of the blade nick his throat as he swept his arm beneath it. The blade flicked out again, as fast as it had flicked in. Kotaro was not to be caught off balance, whirling past Alec as a bull whirls past its matador.

Alec knew, with the sword in Kotaro's hands, his success was only a matter of time. The gleaming tip travelled the shortest distance to his throat. His arm had to move all the way along the perimeter of a semi-circle. Fast though he was, he knew Kotaro was faster. Again the sword, and this time the cut deeper. It flicked out beyond his grasp. His back was almost against the door leading into the computer annexe. If only he could get in there, and through into the computer room itself! But then Kotaro came in again – his point suddenly diverting lower. The change of direction caught Alec, who cast his right arm too high and missed the blade. His left arm quickly up was too late; the blade stuck an inch into the flesh below his left clavicle. Sword quickly out again, and blood spurted. Curiously there was no pain. The last movement had driven him backwards, and suddenly he felt the electric light switch between his shoulders. He lunged forwards, taking Kotaro by surprise. The sword point was deflected downwards as Kotaro pushed his weight backwards, but Alec's desperate movement had made him vulnerable and Kotaro stuck the sword point into his side, aiming for his heart. The point went into the flesh below Alec's upraised arm, running along the side of his rib cage. This time, there was a searing pain and Alec knew he would lose consciousness in minutes. He whirled round, carrying the sword point with him, snapping it free of the cane as his hands found the electric light switch on the wall, plunging the room into instant darkness. There was the sound of running feet which Alec tried to follow, the door opened and light came in from the room beyond. Alec tried to hold the door but felt himself losing consciousness. Frank sprang to his feet as soon as the light went out, came rushing at the door but in the gloom crashed into Alec's body and sent him head first into the door which slammed shut again. By the time Frank managed to drag Alec's unconscious body away from the door, Kotaro was nowhere to be found.

## PHASE 30

Sally and Samuel Reynolds were by Alec's side in the quality check room when he recovered consciousness. The wounds on his throat and in his side had been dressed by the first-aid man at the plant, and the Company doctor was expected at any minute. He struggled upright, wincing with the pain in his side.

'You were very lucky,' Sally said, trying to push him back down again on the table top. 'If that wound in your side had deflected the other way off your ribs, the sword would have gone straight into your heart.'

'I haven't got one,' Alec said, his humour rising grimly to the surface.

Frank Lester stepped forward, looked at Samuel Reynolds as he spoke to Alec. 'I carried you out of there, down on to the blast furnace floor and out here without anyone seeing me.'

'Good man!' Alec said, but there was no smile on Frank's face.

'While I was doing it,' he said glumly, 'I'm afraid Peter Reynolds must have recovered, and he got away.'

Alec looked at Samuel Reynolds. He had aged ten years since the previous morning, when Alec had told him Peter was suspected. Together they had examined Peter's bedroom, and it was Alec who found the radio transmitter, hidden by the hardboard sheet which blocked up the front of an old-fashioned coal fireplace.

166

'They must still be in there,' Samuel Reynolds said.

'No one's come past my men,' the Captain added. 'And they've been on watch every minute since you went inside.'

Alec struggled upright. 'We'll wait for daylight,' he said, 'then we'll look for them. They must be in there somewhere.'

The night was long, and bitterly cold. At times the temperature dropped to fourteen degrees below freezing. Alec noticed the overhead railway had stopped. 'I ordered it stopped,' Samuel Reynolds said, 'in case the pulleys should freeze. This must be the coldest night we've had for fifty years!'

The awful frozen night set in. The canteen staff made a thermos urn of coffee which, mounted on a trolley, was pushed from soldier to soldier. The computer control team carried on – Alec hadn't informed them that their major secret had been stolen, and the master tape now carried no record of the furnace programmation. During the night, the maintenance men made several brews of tea, and they ate the sandwiches they had brought with them. Since a lavatory was attached to the control room itself, no one had reason to leave. At seven o'clock in the morning the day shift would come on duty. The furnace was working satisfactorily and had been tapped off twice during the night. The pig-iron it had made had already gone to the Bessemers for blowing into steel, and rolling the first ingot was due to start at four o'clock that afternoon.

Alec refused to go to bed, though Samuel Reynolds offered him the hospitality of his house. He lay where he was on the table in the quality control room. Sally stood beside him for a long time, holding his hand.

'Did you mind me sending for you?'

'No, I was glad to come, if you needed me!'

'I made you a promise in Japan!'

'I asked you to.'

'I wanted you to be here when I carried it out. There's not sufficient evidence to call in the police, but I'm absolutely certain in my own mind Peter Reynolds killed your father.'

Sally looked at Samuel Reynolds, the man she had worked for, had come to understand so well. She put out her hand, and touched his arm. It was hard for him to speak, but: 'I believe that, too,' he said, 'from what Mr Haig has told me, and from what I have seen tonight. There's nothing I can say about it. I can and will take care of all the material things for you and your mother and family, but that does nothing to help bring your father back, does it?'

'If it's any comfort to you – and I know this is a hard thing to say – some people are better off dead. My father was never a very happy man.'

'Peter was never a very happy boy!' The Old Man turned away.

Alec reached out and grasped Sally's hand, and pressed it. 'Go and get some sleep,' he urged. 'We shan't do anything until morning, and I promise to call you. Take Mr Reynolds with you.'

She went up to the Old Man, and after a few words he went with her.

Alec finally got up off the table-bed. They had laid a mattress on it, brought from the office women's rest room, and he was wrapped in blankets. The doctor came, looked at the wounds, said there was nothing he could do except order Alec into hospital for treatment against shock. When Alec refused to go, he gave him an anti-tetanus injection, prescribed lots of hot sweet tea, and as little movement as possible.

Without the noise of the overhead railway the place seemed deadly quiet – the rumble of the blast furnace and the Bessemers subdued in the night air. The wind whistled across

168

the empty spaces of the steel works, where few of the enormous sheds had doors. About four o'clock it started to snow again.

The snow must have come through the air from warmer skies above the icy blanket – it dropped heavy and filled with slush. As soon as the snow touched the ground, it set hard. Now the soldiers were beginning to feel the effects of the frost, and several complained of frozen feet. One of them asked the permission of his officer to break up an old packing case near by – the officer referred it to the Captain who referred it to Alec, and soon a ring of fires had started all round the blast furnace shed.

'Now no one could possibly get out,' the Captain said. The fires gave a ring of illumination impossible to pierce unseen.

Shortly after the day shift had taken over, and the night shift had been permitted through the cordon, daylight came. Alec stood up, testing his legs. He felt a little weak from loss of blood, but no one would have known it from his crisp manner. 'Right,' he said. 'We'll go in and get them!'

The Captain withdrew half the men from the cordon and they started systematically to examine every square foot of the blast furnace shed.

At eleven o'clock Alec had to admit it. Not a trace of Kotaro Hitohori nor Peter Reynolds could be found.

# PHASE 31

The cable railway started about a quarter-past eleven, tipping on to the lower level. Morgan Morgan, Frank Lester's successor, was sitting in the cab of his bulldozer, smoking, looking down on the half-filled tubs as each one came in succession along the cable way, to be tipped by the tipper arm on to the top of the small slag heap he would soon have to spread. Suddenly, he jumped out of his cab into the icy air, ran to the gantry at the top of the pit hill, pressed the button that stopped the cable railway, seized the telephone and shouted into it.

Alec drove like a madman up the hill, Samuel Reynolds in the car with him, despite Alec's protest. When they got there, Morgan Morgan had placed a ladder against the side of the ore tub, ten feet in the air above the lower level. The ore tub was about five feet diameter, and five feet deep, made of cold solid iron. Looking down the length of the wire Alec saw how close the wire passed to the back of the blast furnace shed. It would need a jump of only three feet for anyone standing on the arm which jutted from the shed. Inside, they were sitting in the bottom of the tub, huddled together, doubtless for warmth. They had frozen solid during the night, during that long bitter freezing night when the Old Man stopped the cable railway and left them stranded, in the tub, four hundred feet in the air above the valley bottom, with icy wind breathing its frozen blasts on the cold iron sides, blowing over the rim of the tub, sucking out the last vestige of body heat from the two men huddled, unprotected, on the slag.

Alec climbed into the tub. The Old Man climbed the ladder, looked inside for a hard minute finally to verify with his own eyes that his son was there, and then climbed down the ladder, walked off the tip hill, and away over the moors above the valley.

When Alec came down, Morgan Morgan was standing at the foot of the ladder, shaking with the Welsh fear of the supernatural, death and dying, the horror of the ghosts.

'They stole some papers,' Alec said ' – and towards the end, they had to set fire to them to give themselves warmth to live for another five minutes. They also had a computer tape – but that wouldn't burn.'

'Why?' Sally asked. 'Why? I can understand with a man like Kotaro Hitohori, but what was there in it for Peter Reynolds?'

They were in Alec's room in the hotel. The steel works was back to normal, if ever it could be that way. Instecon had given a gift of a pound note to each soldier before he left the camp, and the computer was busily turning out steel under Ianto's happy and benevolent guidance. Samuel Reynolds had come back to the house within the steel works gate, but Alec had caught him leaving with a small suitcase.

'Where are you going?' Alec asked.

The Old Man tried to brush past him, but Alec blocked his path. 'Running away from the works won't help you or Instecon,' Alec said. 'Sodaberg's needed in Copenhagen where we have much worse trouble than here, and someone's got to run this plant!'

There were tears in the Old Man's eyes. 'I know what you're trying to do, Mr Haig, and it speaks well for your humanity, but I never could. You'd never trust me, ever again, and I'd never trust myself . . .'

'That's a load of balls!' Alec said, with deliberate brutality. 'Your family has cost us a lot of time, effort and money, Mr Reynolds, and it's up to you to take your coat off again and get stuck in, to pay some of that time and effort and money back! That sulphur content on the third shift of the coke oven is still no better, and I'll be damned if I'm going to waste my time hanging about here finding out which of the oven men is lacking at his job. There's the Bessemer to be automated and though Ianto may be the most brilliant computer expert we've got, he'll make a bloody mess of installing a computer on the Bessemer unless we have a real steel man to back him up.'

The tears had dried from Samuel Reynolds's eyes. 'Are you speaking for the board?' he asked.

'I was on the telephone to Zürich not half an hour ago,' Alec lied, 'and they gave me hell about that sulphur content!' Alec grabbed his arm, turned him, and walked back up the path with him towards the house. 'Your main problem here, Mr Reynolds,' he said, 'is the low yield on capital employed. Now, if you could examine the production volume in terms of man hours, you'd see that . . .'

'Here, are you trying to teach me my job?' the Old Man said gruffly. He grasped Alec's hand and shook it. 'Thanks, anyway,' he said.

Alec turned round to leave him, somewhat hesitant.

'I'm all right now!' the Old Man said. 'But there is one thing you can do for me. If ever you find out why Peter did it, come and see me, and tell me, no matter how bad it is. If I was the cause of it, if I brought him up wrongly, I'd like to know. It'd be a bit easier to bear if I knew the mistake was mine, not his!'

Alec left him there, and came straight back to the hotel. As usual when a case was solved, he felt an unbearable lassitude descend upon him. Now the pain of his several wounds combined to sap his energies. He was in bed in the hotel when Sally found him.

'It's no good asking me why!' he said. 'That's something no one will ever know!'

'And now you go back to Zürich and wait for the next job,

for the next time somebody wants to stick a knife or fire a bullet into you!'

'This job isn't finished yet. Tomorrow I go back to Tokyo.'

There was a look of dismay on her face, of anguish for him. 'When do you leave?'

'Ten o'clock in the morning.'

'And how do you plan to spend the rest of your time here in South Wales?' she asked, a glint in her eyes.

'Where Frank Lester is spending his day off – in bed!'

# PHASE 33

It was night time as the plane carrying Alec Haig on the southern route flew along the Tokyo waterfront before banking for the turn over Tokyo Bay that would put it down at Haneda. The lights atop the Tokyo Tower – thirteen metres taller than the Eiffel Tower – winked out over the city, but there was no welcome in them for Alec. He was the last passenger to leave the plane. When he came down the steps, he was wearing an airline mechanic's overalls, and a flat cap hid much of his face. Somehow he seemed to have shrunk below his normal six feet one. Katsuhiro Kai had gone on to the plane – together in an airlines Datsun they drove through the back gate. Alec without luggage didn't go through Customs. On the far side of the tarmac Antonio Giovanni waited in a four-seater Bell helicopter. Within minutes of Alec's arrival they took off and flew straight out over Tokyo Bay. It was a clouded night, and little could be seen of the water below them. The pilot of the helicopter knew exactly where he was going and put them down a few minutes later on the other side of a hill from the Mitziguchi steel works. A waiting Datsun carried them swiftly over the hill. They left it about a quarter of a mile from the high wall around the steel works and walked quickly through the symmetrical paths criss-crossing the rice paddy extending to the walls. When they arrived Antonio took a short tube from his pocket and, twisting it, erected a stiff, hollow pole twenty feet long. On the top of the pole he clipped a small box with two tensile steel hooks protruding from the top. From the box hung a few inches of nylon cord, fastened to a leather strap. A thin nylon cord extended from this strap. He lifted the pole and hooked the box neatly on top of the wall. Then he and Katsuhiro took hold of the thin cord attached to the leather strap and pulled it down. Alec stepped forward, put his foot in the strap, and Antonio released the thin cord he held. The pull of the hydraulic mechanism in the box quickly raised him level with the wall top. He swung a leg along, taking care not to expose himself along a skyline to anyone on the other side. He wriggled along to make way for Antonio.

Once inside, they walked around the perimeter, Antonio leading the way in deep shadow along a path that seemed little used, so uneven was its surface. Soon they came to the back of the blast furnace shed. Waiting on a railway siding were trucks to take molten pig iron to the Bessemers. They cut through the railway sidings, hiding beneath trucks whenever one of the shunting workers came into the railway yard, and after about a half mile, Antonio dropped back.

'How's your side?' he asked Alec.

'Don't concern yourself about it!' Alec said, annoyed Antonio should think him potentially weak. 'Which way now?'

Before them the brilliantly lighted yard outside the Bessemer plant extended five hundred yards. The overhead lights revealed the men working in the yard, which was crisscrossed with roads and railway tracks and enormous pipelines about ten feet from the ground that carried the main water and steam supplies.

Antonio beckoned to him and they drew back into the shelter of a building. It was lucky for Alec he couldn't read the Japanese slogan – 'Danger: extreme high voltage' – painted on the door. A pipeline two feet in diameter came across the earth towards this building, where it reared twenty feet into the air to cross the yard. The pipeline had another about a foot in diameter above it, and the sides of the two pipelines were boxed in. Antonio pointed upwards and then started to climb. Alec circled his hands around the pipeline below Antonio and followed. Half-way up he leaned back to rest against the foot-thick pipeline behind him. It was filled with super-heated steam! When he got to the bend on the pipeline he saw Antonio squirming his way along inside the tunnel between the two pipes, limber as a rabbit. There was only about eighteen inches of headroom beneath the pipe carrying the superheated steam. Alec lay flat along the larger pipe and started to squirm forwards. Now he knew why Antonio had insisted on the overalls, since the dust of ages had settled on the surface. Several times, incautiously, he lifted his head, but each time the heat of the pipe above forced it down again. He was wet through before he had gone ten yards, and remembered he had five hundred yards to go. Both feet must be kept above the pipeline to prevent his legs dangling below the protective wooden screen. He kept his feet crossed and moved his ankles as far up as they would come. Then he moved one hand and arm forwards and raised his body. Pulling with the forward arm, and pushing with the other, pressing with his ankles down on the pipe, he was able to straighten his knees and advance his body about eighteen inches. This motion he repeated, over and over again, for five hundred yards.

At the far end of the pipeline they slid down in the shadow of the Bessemer building. Alec felt his thigh tremble where he had been burned, the blood run from the sword wound beneath his clavicle, and along his ribs. As they dropped to the ground his legs buckled, and he sat with his back to the Bessemer building.

Antonio dropped down beside him. 'We go out an easier way!' he said.

As soon as Alec felt able to walk steadily again, they went round the back of the Bessemer shed. There waited vessels for carrying steel from the Bessemer into the ingot casting, a long tall sentry line of gigantic egg-cups, each mounted on its own tipper bogey. It took Alec less than thirty seconds to get into the first. He took with him the gun Toni had made for him so long ago, or so it seemed, in a garage in Zürich. From the far side of the railroad tracks came the rhythmic clank of the ore crushing mill. Over the clamour it made no one could have heard the rhythmic pounding of Alec's gun against the inside of the steel vessel. When he reappeared from the inside, there was an almost beatific smile on his face. He moved along to the next cup, and the next, firing into the inside of each cup three dozen of the small triangular metal pieces. The gun worked on compressed air, and spat its bullets into the inside wall of the vessel with no more difficulty than pushing a finger into butter. When he was half-way down the line Antonio, verifying the time with his watch, signalled to him, then ran down the side of the Bessemer building. He was gone for half an hour, suddenly manifesting himself as Alec climbed out of the last steel vessel. Together they skirted the Bessemer building, and reached the wall. They circled around beneath the wall until they had reached the place they had previously crossed. The time showed exactly five o'clock. The hydraulic ladder suddenly appeared on the top of the wall.

'Thank God!' Antonio said. 'I wasn't looking forward to having to climb up there if Katsuhiro hadn't shown up!'

They crossed the wall, walked through paddy-field paths to where the car was waiting. They didn't talk at all, each busy with his own thoughts. They climbed wearily into the car and were driven rapidly to where the helicopter was waiting. The helicopter took off at once, and headed out over Tokyo Bay. At the airport, Alec, in the hut of the mechanic who had loaned the overalls ·to Katsuhiro, stripped off and washed himself all over in the small wall sink. Then he put on his own clothing and stepped out of the shed, the modern, smart, indistinguishable, international business executive.

Anyone looking at his face, however, and the scar down his cheek, would have been arrested by the grimness of his features. He walked across the tarmac. The plane was already fuelled and they were waiting for passengers for the polar flight to Copenhagen. He had booked the entire front compartment. He took his seat. The stewardess came to him. 'Are you comfortable, sir?' she asked.

'When this plane takes off,' he said, 'I intend to fall asleep, and I intend to stay asleep for fifteen hours until we reach Copenhagen. During this flight, I intend to keep my seat belt fastened all the time, I shall not smoke, so you will not need to tell me to extinguish my cigarette, and I shall not be interested in the piece of paper sent round by the Captain to inform us we are passing over the North Pole. I shall not want waking for meals, I do not wish to purchase duty-free cigarettes, duty-free alcohol or perfume. You may waken me only when you can actually see Copenhagen with your own two lovely eyes! Is that clearly understood?'

'Oh, damn! One of those,' the stewardess thought. 'Certainly, sir, I understand, but is there nothing you'd like before you go to sleep?'

'Yes,' he said. He reached up and kissed her full on the lips.

The plane took off exactly on time, and they were circling out over Tokyo Bay to turn to their northern route when Alec started to chuckle. Those 'nails' he had fired into the steel vessels contained an enormous amount of 'flosflolus', a measurable amount of which would be dissolved in the molten steel every time the vessels were used. The Mitziguchi Company did not normally analyse its steels for phosphorus after the Bessemer sample! They'd be sending out some curious material from now on, as long as the 'flosflolus' bullets lasted!

The tall tower of the Mitziguchi steel works appeared to the starboard side, visible through the porthole by his elbow. He glanced at his watch. The monitoring room would be empty now, all the operatives receiving the morning briefing from whoever had succeeded Kotaro Hitohori. At that moment, the sun glinted on the aluminium bubble on the top of the water tower, its glare high-lighting the word Mitziguchi. The aluminium bubble burst, upwards, into a thousand pieces, the concrete water tower holding the control room beneath it burst, thousands upon thousands of gallons of water were thrown into the air, steam rose from the tower, and the last sight Alec had as he settled back into his seat for his fifteen-hour sleep was the word Mitziguchi, exploding into a thousand small pieces, like the pieces of a jigsaw.

'Well done, Antonio,' he said. 'That evens the score for the coke oven men!' He fell asleep.

The stewardess came along the aisle, gently unfastened his seat belt, and took a blanket from the shelf above him and wrapped it round him.

Then she bent down, and kissed him on the lips.

He opened one eye. 'Thanks!' he said.

INSTECON

INTERNAL MEMORANDUM DISTRIBUTION A. ONLY

From: Head of Accounts

To:    Head of Tech. Sales (Misc.)

Having now taken the opportunity, despite the
heavy volume of work which constantly passes
through this Department, of reading report
AH/TS (Misc.) - Tokyo, we are authorizing
payment of the item previously queried
(Item 17, page 2 - fee to T. C. Pappayannikas
£17. 10. 0d. sterling equivalent). From
the expense account, however, we notice
the purchase (Item 24, page 5) of 'One Kimono,
Shishu-moyo, Crane and Tortoise', which we
believe to be symbolic of 'Happy Couple'.
Since this item does not appear in the report,
we presume it to be a private gift and
therefore deduct the amount of 17,500 yen
(£17. 10. 0d. sterling equivalent).

                    J. C. Crump. Head of Accounts